THE PARADISE FACTORY

CORTEX BOOK ONE

JIM KEEN

**Get Jim Keen's sequel to this book *Contact Binary*
FOR FREE**

Sign up for the no-spam newsletter to get the exclusive CONTACT BINARY novella, unique illustrations, in depth character studies, details about the future history of New York, free 3d models, and more from the Cortex universe all for free.

Details can be found at the end of THE PARADISE FACTORY.

[1]

"Projections from the Pentagon's own Mechanical Intelligence suggest workforce unemployment will reach 90% in the next five years. We recommend the following steps to ensure the United States remains a sovereign entity. First, change the role of military and police forces from external and internal security, to riot suppression and general order control."
Department of Homeland Security and Employment report, "Eyes Only,"
President of the United States, 2048

"Organized crime is the future of law enforcement."
Fox Mangrusso, Five Points captain, New York, 2050

"With development of the Dyson engine, and the resultant cheap aerial transportation, we are now left with the question of what to do

with the bridges and tunnels. My suggestion is to make them law-free zones, areas where anything can be researched. This should prove a significant aid in attracting big business."
New York City Planning Review presented to Mayor Robert Thornley, 2052

NEW YORK, JUNE 22nd, 2055

THE GREAT CITY HUMMED, UNAWARE AND UNCARING, AS ALICE rolled over and spat blood into the snow. Her chest throbbed with the dull pain of broken ribs, a pain that spiked into hot needles when she tried to move. Her police uniform hadn't absorbed the Thumper's full charge, and a disk of melted composites glowed orange as it cooled over her ribcage.

She tried to stand, failed, and slid back to the frozen concrete. New York's meat-locker chill seeped through her clothing and she shivered uncontrollably.

Mike had ten years on the force, and she had four in the Marines, yet they'd just been jacked like rookies. The stun round had taken him head on, its wet *thok* echoing from the brickwork as anesthetic gel smothered his face. He'd been unconscious before he hit the ground, the Thumper putting her down seconds later.

Alice looked over at the ambush site—there was no blood, no equipment, just two sets of military boot prints separated by heavy drag marks. Whoever hit them knew where they were headed, and how to separate them from the NYPD surveillance drones. To do that required data—*privileged* data.

"Suit, where's Mike?"

"You mean Officer Squire?"

The dry, male voice came from the collar of her bulletproof jacket, its lining buzzing with every word. She didn't bother to answer, just let the pain ebb from her body.

"Be like that then," the voice continued. "As for *Mike*, how should I know? He's exceeded my tracker range. This whole situation is your fault. I said not to come in here, but did you listen? Did you? Of course not. Too busy playing the hero. Well, look where that has got you. Come on—hurry up, hurry up, before we both lose our jobs."

Alice counted to five, then pushed herself onto her knees and stood. Snow formed a lumpen grid over the broken ground, its geometric pattern created by bird capture nets strung between the buildings. She pulled a stim-stick from her suit, jammed the glass pipe in her mouth, and inhaled its bitter powder. A second later her heart thrashed as if wired to a fusion reactor and her vision cleared. *That's good shit,* she thought, but her body was rubbery and remote. There was a payback coming when this wore off, a tsunami lurking over the horizon.

Her riot gun jutted from the snow, an LED on its front cartridge flashing red. She exhaled and picked it up. The weapon was cheap mass-produced plastic, its gray sides embossed with red Cantonese hieroglyphics. She clipped it to her tactical sling, then typed into her wrist keypad. Its small screen rendered the surrounding streets as green cubes over a black background, but there was no sign of Mike.

"See? I told you that *Mike* was out of subcutaneous tracker range. Now, if it's not too much trouble, why don't you locate him on foot?"

Awesome, I'm taking orders from my clothing now, Alice thought, but did as instructed and limped back up the street.

THE ALLEY HAD BEEN WELL CHOSEN. It zigzagged from the city's street grid to end in a cul-de-sac hidden from anyone except building residents. They'd missed the ambush warning signs coming in here, too intent on running down the kid waving a shrapnel gun. The structures on either side were empty; once grand town houses now nothing but roofless soot-stained brick walls open to the electric sky. A large golden sunflower had been graffitied across one wall, the paint dripping in long streaks; the rest were bare.

Alice followed the drag marks. The snow was heavy in places, the wind forming tall drifts at the foot of each building. Mike had been taken west, the buildings changing from broken homes to patched-up squatter units ideal for ambush. Tribeca had been one of the last neighborhoods to empty out, but once the Ones fled to the towers, the void left behind sucked in the homeless. New York had thirty million unemployed existing with no social services. Every day tens of thousands lost their homes and found themselves out on the streets with no way back. Fractured windows peeked through corrugated sheeting, once-polished doors stood nailed shut. Fires glimmered inside the ruined structures, the crackle of burning wood, the stink of molten plastic strong in the air. The houses were being torched room by room, anything to hold off the lethal chill.

Alice slowed; she had to check roof lines, windows, and doorways for gang members with bad attitudes and weaponry. Another corner, hard right, opening into a street filled with festering piles of garbage. Tires smoldered, choking black smoke veiled the uplit clouds to create a gray twilight. Alice paused, rubbed her chest, and considered her options. Slowly, the sounds of her movement masked by the crackling tires, she inched to the end of the road and kneeled. *One, two.* She snapped her head around the corner.

The street ran a whole block west, the four-story buildings silhouetted against the storm clouds. It was empty but for a collection of feral dogs howling at her smell.

Then she saw the body crumpled halfway down, unmoving.

Was it time to call Dispatch? No, Mike had used their three allocated calls today, and any further correspondence would be deducted from her salary. Besides the NYPD's new MI—Mechanical Intelligence—would just say *no proof, no backup,* whatever shit a cop found themselves in.

"Suit? Any tracker pickup yet?"

"Yes," her collar speaker said. "Officer Squire's locator is sixty-three feet from our current location."

"Ever feel like telling me?"

"You never listen, so I didn't see the point."

Alice sucked air and tried to calm herself. Her jacket had a Type 3 Mind, so wasn't sentient per Turing ratios, but its consciousness-emulation systems were near perfect. Just her luck it was a prissy asshole.

"Okay, new rules. You can talk if it will save my life."

"I promise to try, but you have to listen as well. It's not like I want to be here. I requested work in a space suit, did I ever tell you that? Just my luck I ended up down here with you."

"Yeah, you told me." Alice ground her teeth in frustration and let the stims push away fatigue. She reached into a small pocket on her left hip. The camera drone was the size and shape of a black marble. She squeezed until it beeped, then threw it high into the air. It wobbled, emitted a low-pitched chatter, then shot toward the prone body. Alice pulled her visors from an inside pocket. The left lens was split in two, but she donned them anyway. They sagged to one side as the right lens stuttered to life, snowstorm interference pixelating before it became a recognizable video feed. The drone showed her an augmented world view—the street ripped past in a blur, visible light supplemented by crimson infrared hotspots and cyan millimeter-wave radar.

The drone spotted nothing but old cobblestones and thick ice until it reached the tangled body. Except it wasn't a body, it was a discarded NYPD jacket and pants surrounded by the contents of Mike's pockets. There was no sign of his service weapon or badge. Both would fetch Obamas on the black market, and losing either was grounds for immediate contract termination. It looked like Mike would be joining the three hundred million unemployed even if Alice did get him back. She hoped he'd saved enough to get by, but with hyperinflation, who knew what that was anymore?

Alice steered the drone around the clothing, and watched the video feed as its small mechanical mind identified the scattered objects, labeling each with a virtual tag. The police barely controlled these streets, and the jackers knew the NYPD paid a large reward for rescuing a kidnapped cop. To stop another gang trying to grab Mike, they'd stripped him to his thermals so he looked like just another loser having a bad day.

The drone beeped a low-battery warning, but Alice kept it looking for tracks until it fell to the ground with a sad squawk. Nothing. The trail was as cold as the air.

She rechecked the rows of dead houses either side of the street looking for snipers or gang members. Internal fires cast dancing shadows against the peeling walls, but revealed no hidden figures. The terracotta parapets ran straight and empty, no surveillance posts or watchmen that she could see. In the background, mile-high Blade Towers rose like mutated carbon trees to fade into the sky.

It was time.

Alice shouldered her riot gun and toggled to wide disperse; the centrifuge spun up with a faint whine. The front cartridge held aluminum pellets, lethal close up, but their limited range wouldn't reach the building rooftops. Still, it might slow a casual attacker enough to give her cover. She breathed in, ignored the pain in her ribs, and sprinted along the southern wall, minimizing her silhouette. Her footsteps crunched, the month-old layers of snow cracking like cheap wood to ghost her progress.

No one moved. The road was silent, dead.

Alice ran until she was parallel to the jacket and stopped, her breath hitching. It was *good* to be in trouble again; adrenaline spiking, mouth dry and sour. Urban warfare had always been her favorite part of Marines basic training, and her upbringing on these very streets had been perfect preparation. That training had been wasted during the last year of crowd control and food-line supervision. She wiped sweat from her face, pulled long black hair into a tight knot, and checked her uniform was zipped closed.

Nobody moved on the street or rooftop, so she ran to the pile of clothing and powered down the drone. She put the machine in her pocket to recharge, swung the riot gun to her back, and picked up the jacket. It was Mike's: his service number glowed on the collar. Anything of real worth had been taken from its pockets, leaving just the odd assortments of life behind: a pen, his old wedding ring, a dented can of Stun Fun. No blood, no signs of a struggle, nothing.

Pros had hit them, she was sure of that now. Maybe Fourth Ward overspill, or ex-cartel up from the Southern Wall. Whoever they were, it was time to make the call. She lifted her arm, ran a credit check, winced at her low bank balance, then called Central Dispatch.

"Dispatch, this is Officer Alice Yu, Badge Number 23-3965-AN. Suspected kidnapping in progress of Officer Michael Squire, Badge Number 77-9667-BT. Backup requested at my location."

"Confirmed, Officer Yu. Be advised the costs of this call are being deducted from your designated credit balance. Now please provide evidence of said kidnapping charge." The MI's voice was calm, well mannered, and sounded utterly human. Even now, a year since the switch, Alice found it hard to believe she was talking to a foot-square brass cube in a refrigeration tank. A cube that consisted of trillions of nanoscopic gears, rods, and pulleys thrashing away to create a believable simulation of the human consciousness.

"I saw it happen, okay? I took a Thumper and by the time I could stand Officer Squire was long gone. I followed drag marks to my current location and found his discarded uniform." She waited, fizzing with adrenaline, as the machine ran its precognition branches.

"Your hypothesis carries an eighty-seven percent probability," it said. "However, under current financial constraints, ninety percent or better is required before additional funds can be released for rapid-response backup."

Alice took a breath, then tried again. "Please clarify evidence required to cross ninety percent threshold."

"Digital recordings of said event, or verifiable witness statements."

"You're not leaving me many options here. I have no footage of the incident, and if I canvas for witnesses there'll be no chance of catching up with the jackers."

"That is an assumption, not a fact. You are directed to proceed on foot and look for the additional evidence required."

Alice muttered a long and colorful stream of words as she closed the signal and took off her visors. She would have to do this solo for now.

The trail was harder to follow than before, but her drone had recharged and with its help she followed the tracks for another two blocks. Then snow started, heavy flakes that swirled around her like a system crash, making the small aircraft unusable.

The jackers had waited until a storm was incoming before they set the trap, knowing the weather would take out aerostat surveillance. These were definitely not your usual perpetrators out to impress employers with their go-to attitude. What the hell was going on here?

The snow thickened; visibility fell to a few feet.

The trail faded, faded, vanished.

Alice looked at the wrecked houses, the burning trash, and the feral dogs gauging whether or not she was weak enough to take down. Play this wrong, she'd lose her job and be living here in a week.

[2]

"Look, I ain't stupid, I sees it comin'. Automation stuff made a dent in the numbers, but didn't break us, right? It was them damn MIs that smashed it all up. Once you plugged one of them into the big board, who needs workers?"
John Rogers, unemployed loader, Bethlehem Nuclear Fusion, PA, USA, 2049

―――

"I lose my house on July 4th. Supposed to be the coldest day of the year as well. Gonna need a better coat. And life."
Tom Ridley, unemployed biochemist, San Francisco, CA, USA, 2051

―――

THIS IS YOUR LAST CHANCE, KEEP YOUR MOUTH SHUT, DO AS YOU'RE told, or you'll never see her again.

Red forced himself to stand still and smile at the Professor.

"Your turn boy—three, two, one, *go*," the Professor, Harvard graduate, Cortex Employee #28, and the Crazy Horse's current bartender, spoke with the tone of an annoyed college lecturer. Drunken laughs echoed from the beer-soaked walls, cheering Red's misfortune.

That old fuck-buzzard loves an audience when there's mail to deliver, Red thought.

The Horse was like a million other dead-end dives: a worn-out bar along one wall, tables opposite, small games room to the rear. Red stood next to a battered pool table alongside nine other street kids plucked from the line outside the building. The brick walls glistened with condensation behind an array of old, curled photographs in bronze frames. Most were black-and-white pictures of boxers, worn faces mugging for the camera.

Red knew the feeling.

Thirty drunken, leering jeeks—street-trash—stood between Red and the outdoors, their gaunt faces haloed by the window's frost-white glow. They all looked the same to him, teeth bared with the joy of someone else's misfortune. A pressed-tin ceiling spanned overhead, hundred-year-old metal sheeting beneath layers of green and brown paint. Red's huge boots added six inches to his height; if he reached up, setting the chains of his ancient leather jacket jangling, he could touch that surface, scratch his name there, make his mark on the world.

As if.

Red knew he was in a barter situation, not some rite-of-passage shit. He shrugged, his oversized black clothing a sack over his emaciated frame. Act too eager and he'd kiss goodbye to any remaining negotiating room.

"Give me the delivery and I'll fix your street sign," he said.

There was a moment's silence, then a deafening cheer filled the bar; beer sloshed upward only to return as stinking amber rain. The Professor's pigeon chest swelled, and he smiled, skull visible beneath waxen skin. "Would you, now? Enlighten me regarding which issues pertain to its function and appearance?"

"Been out at night? Recent, like?" Red knew the Professor hadn't; no one went out at night.

"Of course not—I have this establishment to keep afloat."

Red took his chance and stepped forward, the soles of his huge boots sticking to the beer-stained boards. His dyed red hair jutted upward in spikes, the tips adding horns to the shadow he cast across the floor. "Either the neon's older than Mars, or you got wiring issues. Been strobing like gunfire for weeks, scare any upstanding 'dult away from this hole. I can fix that for you."

Red watched the Professor's mouth grow thin and curl down, emotions easy to read. The old lizard did not like this one bit; getting called out in his own bar by some skinny runt would not stand.

"One assumes you have brought your electrical-engineering degree with you? Something I can peruse to guarantee your bona fides?"

Red raised his arms, hands out, submissive. "No sir. But I grow food in my uncle's window, berries and that, for the Ones. Word got out, and the jeeks kept trying to break in. I rigged a cage around the plants, connected it to a solar pack, and they got melted hands. Sourced the parts all over, Fourth Ward, uptown. Taught myself how to do it."

"If that was such a resounding success, then why are you here?"

"Winter, see? No sun, no crops, need a job."

"What about your schoolwork?" The Professor knew Red had quit school months ago and was making a point of his low standing.

"Don't teach electricals in school, do they? Anyways, my rig is a damn sight more complex than some aged-out wires in a sign."

The Professor raised his arms and the crowd silenced; drunken faces stretched from barstools and wet tables to watch the verdict. He rolled down his sleeves with care, made an exhibition of tying the silver cufflinks, then flexed his fist open and closed. Down or up? Red's heart thumped so hard he couldn't hear.

The thumb emerged level, then rotated up.

Riots.

Cheering.

Look straight ahead—don't crack now. Red made his face a stone mask. *You done nothing yet 'cept make eight lifelong enemies.* The kids lined up against the worn brick wall stared at him with hatred. He pushed them from his mind and walked to the Professor.

"Give it," Red said, snatched at the envelope, missed.

"Three hours for the delivery, boy. It has to be there by six, not a minute more. Understand? No second chances, no late arrivals. This is important."

The Professor lowered the cream-colored envelope. Red hesitated for a moment, then took it. When was the last time he'd held anything man-made? Maybe his uncle's wool blanket. That was crude, though, old and cheap. This was different: hard edged, rectangular, sealed with a thick blob of wax embossed with the Professor's sigil—two circles around a central dot. Red turned it over. His filthy hands had already defaced it; a thumb print smeared the virgin paper. His cheeks flushed; the stupid kid who didn't wash his hands.

He looked at the address. The handwritten script was delicate, beautiful and clear.

For personal delivery to:
Charles Takamatsu,
Cortex Intelligent Machines Inc.
1357 Broadway,
Suite 405,
Manhattan

It was hard to know which was the bigger shock; that this wrinkled old reptile knew the most important person in the world, or that the delivery was to an actual business address on the *island*.

No one trusted digital communications anymore. Cortex's analytical engines were just too good at listening in. If it was urgent, it was hand delivered—and that's where street runners came in. Red had assumed this mail drop was a note to a local bodega or something unimportant. It wasn't.

This was an audition for talent.

Sweat ran under his jacket, his skin slick against its cold lining; a strong, bitter odor rose from his filthy T-shirt. If he could do this, and get a few more runs, he'd earn enough to bring his mom home once and for all, maybe even get a place where his uncle could stay over.

But three hours to Manhattan was impossible, more so with such a precious cargo. Word would be out, and he'd be tagged the whole way, local gangs beating on him to steal it.

The Professor watched him with arched eyebrows; Red hid his confusion and shoved the letter into a pocket.

"When did you write this?" Red said.

"I forget. Five, six hours ago?"

"And you made me wait until I can't make it? I've no chance in three hours. This ain't no fair test."

"Look at me." The Professor swept a stick-thin arm around the room. "Think this is fair, do you, boy? I helped build the first Mechanical Intelligence. Think after what I did, the money I earned for someone else, this is all I deserve?"

"No sir." *Maybe you should have thought of that before you built it, not after.*

The Professor slumped onto a stool. In a moment he aged, skin wrinkling to leave behind an old man with no future. He met Red's gaze with a haunted look. "You can't go back, boy, ever. Let no one tell you otherwise. The only thing we have agency over is our future. Now, name the delivery price or I shall revise my selection."

Red thought of the biggest number he could, one that would change his life if he played it well.

"Ten dollars." His voice betrayed him at the last, hope cracking it.

The Professor's laugh was bitter and cold. "I think we can

manage that." He stood, rummaged behind the bar, and held up an old paper note. "Five dollars for successful completion of delivery."

"Hey, ten, ten."

"Five now, five on delivery." He handed it over. "Now you there, listen up." The old man turned to the other girls and boys in the lineup. Their tattered clothing and blended layers of dirt formed a unified whole. At the Professor's beckoning, they shuffled forward. "This boy, Red, has a letter for Manhattan delivery. He has five dollars in cash in his pocket. I don't care who delivers the letter, in fact I—"

Red sprinted for the door, dragged it open, and was gone, his huge boots sliding over the frozen snow. A staccato rattle clattered behind him as the door was shoved open another eight times.

"Remember, boy, you can never go back," the Professor shouted from behind as Red pushed harder, faster, and ducked into an alley. The East River's icecap glittered white in the afternoon sun as thick snow fell.

Red rounded another corner too fast, and crashed to the ground with a bang that rattled his whole body, a bolt of pain shooting upward from his ankle. He struggled upright, blood in his mouth, and set off again, half a block ahead of his pursuers.

He had no idea how to get to the island, let alone make midtown in a couple of hours.

[3]

"Now that the government has officially canceled all social security, welfare, and Medicaid programs, something else will rise to fill the void. In the past that was organized crime, and we are seeing key indicators that a regrouping is occurring in Brooklyn, Queens, and Staten Island."
Julian Nicole, "Challenges Facing the New York Police Department" presentation to Mayor Thornley, New York, 2052

"Sure, the mortality rate will be high, but the whole point of a law-free research zone is we can kill as many as we need to get it right. The taxes we pay ensure no blowback on us."
Carrol Wardens, CEO, Signal Pharmaceuticals, Boston, 2053

ALICE MOVED THROUGH SNOWFALL SO HEAVY SHE COULDN'T SEE ten feet ahead. Flakes settled on her jacket; white ones that melted, gray ones that left an oily residue and reeked of fat. The gray-storm was overspill from a furnace chimney, the owners using the storm to hide their actions.

There was only one place around here that turned bodies into ash.

The Bridge.

That rusting hulk, once a symbol of New York prosperity, had become Fourth Ward's headquarters and home to its fearsome leader, Piggy Bank.

Mike had been taken by one of the Bridge's snatch crews. It made so much sense Alice cursed herself for not realizing sooner. She hunkered down and opened her mouth to hear better, a tactic learned during Marines basic training. There was her whistling wartime tinnitus—such a part of life she didn't notice it unless she was paying attention—and behind that the faint clamor of people. Voices talking and shouting; animal calls, birds, cows; the grinding of heavy machinery, gritted cogs sucking and pulping.

She crossed to the nearest wall and wiped away a crust of ice covering an enameled sign held in place with steel bolts. The text was clear, printed with large yellow lettering:

—

You Are Now Entering The Fourth Ward Protective Zone.
The Brooklyn Bridge, and its associated environs, are under the oversight of Mr. Bank and the Fourth Ward.
All inhabitants are required to follow the local charter rules.
Failure to comply will result in immediate termination.

—

HEY ASSHOLE
Don't go crying to the cops.
You fuck around and we will cut you up,
sell the good parts, burn the rest.
THIS IS YOUR ONLY WARNING

—

Below that an embossed golden sunflower caught the dim light. She'd only heard of Piggy Bank going after rival gang members, or some recalcitrant supplier, before. His scope had changed, and that was a big problem.

Moving past this warning sign would be in direct breach of the NYPD code of conduct, punishable with immediate contract termination. The Fourth Ward's territory spanned from what used to be the Brooklyn Bridge out to Chatham Street to the north, and Spruce Street to the west. Beyond this point, she would be unemployed, with no support, no backup, and no payoff.

She'd heard rumors of certain specialist undercover teams working down here—the ones filled with burnouts and psychos run by Toko Morris, the NYPD's latest golden boy—but for street-meat like her, this was a dead end.

If she gave up on Mike now, however, returned to base and left him to die, she'd never get another partner. Rookies aren't allowed to patrol alone, so her superiors would stick her on a desk for a month, then fire her for whatever bullshit HR thought up that day.

Alice looked back at the cold street behind her. The wind picked up to tear the snow open. The black tarmac was littered with burning trash; every corner and doorway clotted with huddled groups of unemployed, clothes held together with duct tape.

She had enough money for one more rent check.

She turned to the enameled sign.

Her stomach ached with sour tension.

She looked back again but the snow obscured her view.

If she returned to base she was out of a job; if she went forward she was out of a job.

Or maybe not. Penalties for breaking rules of engagement were severe but discretionary; perhaps Mike could put in a good word for her. If he was still alive, that was.

Get real. He's in as much shit as you are.

The first general-purpose MI had been unveiled only eleven years ago, their vast, alien intelligences replacing mankind at the apex of civilization in a single presentation. Automation followed in a storm that rolled around the planet, obliterating the workforce. Over the last seven years, three hundred million people had lost their jobs across mainland America. No jobs meant no taxable income, no taxes meant bankruptcy for the country, and bankruptcy meant no social security or safety blanket. Lose your job now and there was nothing, and no one, to help you. Once your savings ran out, homelessness, starvation, disease and death were inevitable.

A Hopper flew overhead, bearing the dark blue Cortex logo, the hiss of its Dyson engines muffled by the snow. It rose out of view, headed to a Blade Tower, its occupants oblivious to the wreckage below.

"Money for help? Give me a Gipper, I'll carry you outta here?" a voice said.

The young woman was wrapped in bloodied nurse scrubs stuck together with pins. She had no shoes; her body shook so hard her outstretched hand was a blur.

"I'm a cop," Alice said. "Sorry."

"Fuckin' Scorcher," the woman spat, then slipped away into the white air. Alice stared at the swirling hole left behind. She thought of Mike's wife, riddled with cancer held at bay by medicines he bought on the streets. His kids, older than their years, but still so young.

Fuck it.

If she was going to lose her job, she might as well be able to face herself in the morning. Crouching, Alice inched past the sign to enter Fourth Ward's territory, and said goodbye to the last real job she'd ever hold.

———

ALICE DIDN'T KNOW this area of Manhattan. She'd only been on the streets a few months before they designated the Bridge a police no-go zone.

"Suit, when was the last Fourth Ward intelligence report released?"

"No reliable correspondence since official withdrawal one hundred and seventy-three days ago."

"Nothing?"

"Didn't I make myself clear? None I know of."

"Okay. We're entering a crowd zone, so keep quiet until I say."

"Thanks so much for pointing that out, I had *no* idea."

Her jacket's inner lining contained thousands of heating elements that kept her mobile while she worked the frozen wastelands of New York City. They sucked juice though, the batteries lasting eight hours at best, and today was going to grow long. She switched the elements off and instantly cold crept inward from her collar and cuffs. The jacket's outer layers were supple like a rock climber's gear, but woven from bulletproof fibers wrapped around pinhead lights. Those lights enabled it to spell out any warning required; right now it ran the standard NYPD cease-and-desist legal forms. She reached up to her collar and clicked a toggle twice. The jacket went dark. Her weapons were generic enough, being store bought, so she zipped up pockets, removed the wrist keypad and double-checked there were no other tags or markings that would give her away. She looked as much like a cosplay ninja as she could manage at such short notice.

Time to move.

She'd expected Fourth Ward's protectorate to be similar to the rest of the five boroughs, only worse. She was wrong. Silence was the first thing she noticed; most of New York City was a perpetual chorus of screams and sirens. Here, she was cocooned by the soft fuzz of falling snow, the clop of the occasional horse pulling a plastic loading wagon, and the hushed tones of huddled groups spread around fires.

Alice studied the people with more care than she had in months. A product of New York's brutal orphanages and, afterward, a low-level street gang, Alice had thought she was emotionally resilient. Her time on Mars had been physically and mentally devastating, but even so her first few months as a cop had taken its toll. Mike had watched with sympathy as she tried to assist everyone she met, but New York's desperate situation meant she *couldn't* help, that her job wasn't To Protect and Serve anymore, despite what the NYPD's branding said. No, a modern cop was all about riot control—making sure the mile-long lines for tubes of carbohydrate paste kept moving, that the unemployment halls didn't turn into drug dens or brothels. Over the last year she'd built an emotional shield about herself that meant the unemployed became objects to be moved around and little more. To her shame she no longer saw the clotted crowds as people, but as a backdrop, saving her attention for the troublemakers and strong willed who wouldn't follow orders. Real crime—the organized variety that ran New York far more efficiently than the mayor and his staff ever did—was looked after by specialist police divisions kept well away from street-meat like her.

The people here were cleaner and better fed than she was used to; their calorific intake exceeded the emergency rations handed out by the National Guard every morning. Their fires weren't the gasoline-fueled blazes the Brigade spent the whole day chasing either, but smaller, contained by metal funnels Alice hadn't seen before.

She watched as children played outside, snowmen built and kicked down, the process starting over. One boy looked at her, waved, then took a bite from an apple. She'd tried an apple when she was working as a runner, but that was years ago, the memory vague. You could buy printed versions now, but they were too sweet, the texture all wrong; something to do with misalignment of the print heads.

She walked on, looking for tracks, boots cracking black ice that melted to reveal red crystals. She squatted and placed one on her tongue. Rock salt. They were salting the streets down here, making it safe for people to get around. Why hadn't she heard about this before? Why was no one talking about how Fourth Ward had established a haven here?

"Suit, any tracker signals?"

"I would have told you if so."

The snow abated and Alice moved on, the gray flakes transforming to white dots that melted on her face, her tongue. The bull-black sky fractured and yellow sunlight cut through the clouds to dance over the road. There were *Rules and Retribution* signs pasted on every wall, but there were also people, more of them, all moving in her direction.

The next corner opened onto a four-lane road, the intersection rising up to the Bridge entrance. Cars were aerial these days, only the poor and desperate at ground level, and so this urban wilderness had been repurposed. Thin carbon rods rose to hold fractal camouflage nets over the street, the smart fabric held in tension by a complex system of ties and pulleys. As the wind shifted the nets moved across and back again, maintaining a perfect, flat surface. The upper surface would mimic ground level, but alter the image to show burning trash and crowds fighting for scraps of food. This was military tech, and ferociously difficult to buy on the streets; she had no idea how Fourth Ward had sourced it.

The crowd surged toward this covering; there were hundreds, maybe thousands of people on the move. Alice worked her way to one side and stopped, tried to survey her surroundings without drawing attention.

A security checkpoint sat below the canopy, manned by a team of hack-jobs—part human, part reprint. It was hard to tell much more from this distance, and she didn't want to use her visor out in the open. An operation this large, well funded, and organized was bound to have aerostats running facial recognition software and for all she knew they'd already scanned her. Would the Bridge's supervising systems have her biometrics on file? To analyze this number of people it would have to be a smart-system: at least a Type 4, maybe a 5, but not a fully sentient MI. Those cost more than skyscrapers and were all registered with the UN. That meant the security system couldn't make deductive leaps, and was only good at analyzing information it already had. Her military and police records were all encrypted and stored inside uncrackable federal MIs. So—in theory—the only intel out there should be her orphanage and school reports.

In theory.

As for how she would get through the weapons check ... well, that was a different challenge. Everyone around her was carrying products to sell, bulging bags full of anything you could tear from an old building: copper pipes, lights, sticks, broken furniture, and, here and there, the green tufts of real vegetables sourced from window boxes and hidden rooftop gardens.

Alice ran her hands over her uniform. Her pockets were filled with nasty little pieces of equipment, each designed to hurt, maim, or kill, depending upon how much of a jerk the perp was being. She'd bought each piece on the black market; most were illegal but ignored, some only obtainable through off-world contacts. Any self-respecting security guard would pay Obamas just to play with them, let alone purchase.

She looked around. An old plastic bag was half-visible beneath the melting snow. She picked it up, shook off the ice, and took the wide disk of a Bunny Bopper from a back pocket. It was the most invasive device she owned, a shaped-plasma charge that could carve a hole through an aircraft carrier. If the Bridge was off limits to the law —and covered with this level of security—there had to be markets selling more than salvaged house parts and fresh fruit. She dropped the disk into the bag and mentally added weapons dealing to her growing list of offenses.

ALICE BLENDED into the crowd and moved forward; the crush pressed inward, the cloying space full of sweat and cursing. She tilted her head back and inhaled long drags of cold air; exhaled rods of white frost. The shouts and cries around her lessened as the crowd passed beneath the nets, people aware they were entering dangerous ground. Garish animations scrolled across the underside of the taut fabric contrasting with the digital camouflage on the other side. Some of the videos were Fourth Ward propaganda, others from the mayor's office encouraging weapons and medical startups to move to New York: *Test what you want on our bridges, kill who you want in our tunnels, that's no problem in the Big Apple!*

Alice approached the security zone. The hack-jobs guarding it were high-quality work. Each graft looked clean, the blue zip-scars showing no signs of infection or immunosuppressant complications. The guards all had boosted arms—some with legs to match—which suggested bespoke MI designs rather than generic knock-offs. Consistent skin tones, symmetrical lengths, random freckle patterns. If it wasn't for the scars delineating old and new, and the collection of QR codes and DNA registration tags, you wouldn't know you were dealing with a hybrid.

Alice elbowed her way to the edge of the crowd and stopped. The Bridge emerged from the snow like the skeleton of a dinosaur; the ancient stone towers, cables, and rods submerged under a coral reef of new growth. Ducts rose a hundred feet into the air, while vast water pipes traced along the towers and down to the frozen East River, billowing clouds of steam. The structure looked more a factory than ever, some immense bootstrapped machine with an unknown purpose.

Now she understood the NYPD's general order to leave the Fourth Ward alone. The idea that she might stroll in, bop the kidnappers over the head, and walk out was the delusion of a child. A panicked sickness rose in her stomach, fear and uncertainty coming in waves. She had put herself way beyond the line a cop was allowed to tread.

To go back was pointless; to go forward was reckless.

Her heart kicked, adrenaline and stimulants fizzing. Tingling ran across her arms, and she looked at her hands, turned them over and back, the black bulletproof gloves a second skin. She made fists, then stretched her fingers taut, exhaled clouds of fog.

Be true to yourself: get Mike out, or get the evidence to call SWAT in.

Alice elbowed forward, ignoring the curses, until she pushed up against the security barrier. An inch-long mylar aerostat dove toward her, tiny engines screeching, and scanned her face with a thin green laser. An alarm rang out: the throng dispersed as if she were an oil drop in soapy water.

"You," the closest hack-job said, his head a foot and a half above hers. "On the ground, now." He drew a needle gun and sighted along the barrel.

Well, that didn't take long, Alice thought, as she kneeled and raised her hands.

[4]

"Living out here, under the arches, is better than being in there, and ordered around by a forklift truck."
Mark Noble, unemployed warehouse manager, Brooklyn, 2053

"First time it froze was maybes a few inches, but it's got worse with all this new weather. Foot or two now, don't see open water until July, then only for a few months before the snows start again. Shit, be seeing penguins here before too long."
Bill Smicer, Hudson River fisherman, NY, USA, 2054

RED WAS A SKINNY KID, DECENT STAMINA BUT NEITHER FAST nor nimble on his feet. His huge boots pounded the frigid cobbles as shouts came from behind. His outfit wasn't made for sprinting: too tight and heavy. Angular types would have worn runners or something light and sensible, but Red would rather have his legs amputated than wear half the stuff street kids rolled in.

His ankle thumped with a sickening pain as the first bands of a stitch tightened about his chest. He pumped his feet, kept his breathing in check, and skidded around another corner. More shouts from behind, louder, closer. This area of Brooklyn was filled with old warehouses, the tall, graffiti-smothered brick walls crowding in on either side. The ground was an assault course of cracked and peeling tarmac and loops of material bent into trip hazards ready to throw him to the floor once again. A rock shattered against the wall near his head, showering him in sharp fragments. Another street, more clumps of unemployed huddled in corners, shouting at him as he raced past. He cleared a mumbling, semiconscious woman in one long leap, fell down hard, boots sliding on black ice, then up and *go go go*. A scrawny hand grabbed at him from a doorway, missed. Red kept pushing, breath a leaden weight in his lungs, left foot, right foot, *move*.

The pain in his ankle, legs, and chest became overpowering. He staggered to a stop and flashed a look behind: the gang was less than twenty feet away. He gulped air and burst forward, as fast as he could go, putting everything he had into one final sprint to shake them off. He needed a plan, something to give him a break. What to do? He tried to think but his mind looped in panic, the urge to hunker in a doorway and give up pounding him in waves. He'd never see his mom again if he did that; he had to keep going.

Snow flashed onto his skin, across his face, in his eyes. Small white flakes at first, then waxy gray ones that reeked of sour fat. The Bridge was close, its body furnaces fired up. What about there? He'd sold blueberries in its open market a few times, and there were plenty of places to hide if you could sneak onto the main span.

No. If he went there with nothing to sell, the Bridge kids would chuck him off the side, watch him make a red circle on the ice below.

Besides, that whole area was Fourth Ward territory, and so locked down you couldn't even spit on the sidewalk without some 'dult getting in your face about social responsibilities. Last thing he needed was some self-appointed champion of the peace enforcing whatever rules they'd made up that day.

Cold air burned his throat. His feet skipped over the iced cobbles. Another fall or a twisted ankle and it was over.

He gave one final panicked burst of speed, and saw the East River's ice crust bright in the distance. He looked behind him—the gang was closer, lips pulled back in white snarls. In a minute he'd be out in the open and exposed to the local kids. He needed a plan, but exhaustion and fear wouldn't let his mind settle.

Red burst onto the waterfront. Across the ice, Manhattan's Blade Towers rose into the sky, hard and linear trusses lower down, becoming mutated soft structures as they entered the darkening storm clouds. Glittering lines of Hoppers connected them, automated jewels against the leaden sky. Red had been to this area of Brooklyn before, running errands for his uncle, but it had changed since his last visit.

There were more Fourth Ward signs now, their beachhead growing into Brooklyn. The Manhattan Bridge lurked to his right, what used to be the Brooklyn Bridge to his left. Before Dyson engines made local aerial transport commonplace, these riveted dinosaurs carried cars, people, trains. Now anyone with money took Hoppers, snuggled safe in heated seats while children froze in the streets.

Where to go? Where? The Bridge was out, and the Manhattan Bridge was even worse—nothing but a festering half mile of drug distilleries and arms dealerships. The Scorchers would sweep through every month or so to keep their arrest numbers high. Red didn't know what was worse these days—jeeks mashed on the latest chemicals, or the Scorchers acting all superior behind their bulletproof cop gear. His mom was right about one thing: you never, *ever*, trust the police.

"Give it up, stop, don't make me cut you up." The breathless shout was so close Red didn't dare look back, just ran for the river, sweat steaming from him like a racehorse.

He'd seen kids try to make it across the ice a few times before. Not many succeeded. The snow made the entire surface look the same, no way to tell if it was an inch or a mile thick. Red flashed a glimpse at the Bridge. Clouds of fog shrouded the stone towers, while icebergs piled beneath the main span creating a white wall. That, at least, should hold him if he could make it there.

Red reached the river's filthy concrete wall and clambered over, and onto, the ice. His worn rubber soles had no grip and he slid and fell. He pushed himself up as the chasing gang reached the wall. A heavy girl with a broken nose pulled a knife.

"Give it," she said and stepped onto the ice.

Red edged backward, his feet loose under him, arms flailing like sails. "We can talk this out, right?"

She moved in a relaxed skid. "Give it, or I cuts ya."

Red matched her pace, moving away from the shore. The Bridge steamed to his left, icebergs rumbled and cracked as they became wedged underneath its main span. The snow was thick; cold water seeped into his boots as he squelched backward. All he needed to do was—

There was a *crack* beneath his feet. Another, another, then one that was longer and louder. In dreadful slow motion the ice disintegrated, and Red fell through into the poisonous river.

The cold shook Red so hard he gulped a lungful of the oily, black filth. He retched, spat, hands scrabbling for the edge of the ice flow. He went under, came back up, and caught a glimpse of his assailants backing off, mouths open.

"Help me—" he gargled as the tide seized his boots and dragged him under.

———

RED'S MOM had bailed near on a year ago. It was hard to know for sure; it wasn't like he kept a calendar or anything. His uncle took him in without too much fuss. The old horse had his rules, most to do with his music collection, but didn't everyone? If you spend all day, every day, in your apartment it's bound to give you a few kinks.

In those early days the old man treated Red like broken furniture. Only music got him going, old stuff on these big black discs. Red hadn't liked it at first, then he listened to the words, felt hope behind the noise. It was written by kids like him, fucked up and fucked over, music their only way out.

The day uncle Joey gave him an old leather jacket had been the breakthrough. Red painted them cool sound waves from one record on the back, and the ransom-note letters from that other album on the front. Afterward it was better between him and his uncle—not great, but Red no longer felt in the way, and slept on the sofa instead of the floor.

Their apartment was on the fifth floor, its single-leaf brick wall facing south. In the summer it shimmered like a fusion reactor under the inexorable sun. That gave Red the window-box idea, and the fruit sales saved them.

Red looked up at the yellow disk of the sun, its pale fire weak and distant. He couldn't imagine ever feeling warm again, the surrounding cold a relentless force. The sun buckled and warped through the passing ice as the tide dragged him along. He reached up with dead fingers to touch the hard surface as it slid by.

There was a fire in his chest; bubbles rose from his nose to glimmer in the dim light.

His boots were so heavy, the water so black.

Most of all he was sorry; sorry he'd never see his mom again, sorry he'd not learned to play the guitar, sorry he had to die doing something as stupid as mail delivery. How would Uncle Joey cope without Red's income? His mom was certain Joey had money stashed away, but all Red ever saw was an old man living frugally enough to get by.

His arms dragged behind him, his hands bunched into claws.

Blood pulsed in his ears, a thud so loud it he thought his head would split open with it. His lungs burned with the desire to breathe, air pushed at his clamped lips, desperate to be released. It was brighter now, shafts of white light spearing the blackness. This was it—death's hallucinations, the last thrashing of his subconscious.

Then the cold lessened, the impossible numbness replaced with an enveloping warmth. Red looked up to glimpse sky rippling through open water, fishermen waving at him as he drifted past. He half felt, half saw, something vast approaching, and he twisted his body. The Bridge's masonry towers sank away into blackness, while the open mouth of a steel duct belched huge steam bubbles. He pushed upward, kicked with his boots, and his head broke the oily surface. He managed one freezing gulp of air, went under again, then clawed his way back up.

Ice had melted around the ductwork's sides to form a circular pool of water, but the tide was carrying Red past it, and back under the ice. He had seconds, at best. He kicked toward the tower and flailed with his hand. An old, rusted metal ladder had been glued to the stone beside the duct. With his last dregs of energy he grabbed the bottom rung and clung on, half in and half out of the water.

There was nothing for his feet to grip, and the tips of his boots skidded across the submerged stone. A sharp pain grew in his elbow as his weight bore down on the rusted metal. The steam made it hard to breathe, his lungs straining. He squeezed his eyes shut, and stretched upward to find another rung. The metal was hot and wet under his fingers. He gripped, pulled. Again. His whole body shook with the effort, mouth clamped tight, face to the skies, but he repeated the process, arm over arm until his feet found leverage and he lifted himself free of the boiling water.

Red hung there, sucking huge lungfuls of cold air, then vomited black water down his front. The snow was heavier now, the wind freezing—the storm he'd spotted earlier had arrived. He clung to the ladder, life spreading through him with every breath, and looked back at the open water. Maybe he could jump in, swim against the current, then—

No point. The kids from the Crazy Horse were running, skidding, and falling their way toward him. He had to go up and onto the Bridge.

Red summoned what little energy he had left, and pulled himself upward one rung at a time.

[5]

"Some inventions arrive with a bang and are overnight successes. Mechanical Intelligences—MIs—were like that. Once Cortex got their Babbage circuits perfected, those alien life-forms were everywhere. Organic printing is the other kind of invention, the sort built upon years of slow and steady research.
The dream of being able to manufacture human body parts has been around for decades. The first prints were individually modeled on 3D systems, generic and expensive, but life changing to those they helped. Then MIs came on the scene. What had taken thousands of hours by hand could be brute-forced in minutes, and now anything is possible. Full-body reprints, a fountain of youth to the rich, are tightly controlled by the UN's Department of Proliferation Control (D-PRO), and ferociously expensive. Most reprinted owners reside in the towers and, as such, are of little consequence to us. There are simpler ways to upgrade, though—illegal body shops will replace any organ for the right price. There are laws preventing augmentation, but it requires exhaustive tests to determine if an arm is a standard reprint, or an upgrade with titanium bones capable of puncturing your street armor.

Therefore, in stop and search scenarios, it is official policy to shoot first and ask questions later."
Michael Strapson, "Augmentations and Approved Violent Retaliation" NYPD academy class lecture, New York, 2051

ALICE LAY SHIVERING ON THE TARMAC AS THE SECURITY TEAM spread out to surround her. Weapons hummed and clicked as they spun up or sucked power from battery packs. What had tagged her? Was it the retina scan? If so, that meant the NYPD MI had been compromised by Piggy Bank's hacker crew. All the big talk about how analytical engines were foolproof and incapable of error was such bullshit.

She had gear in her suit that could take out the locals, but there was no way she'd be able to handle the aerostats. It only needed one with an active suppression system and any escape attempt would be over before it got going.

I'm sorry, Mike, she thought as the closest hack-job shoved a Glock GS-V handgun into his belt and grabbed her with his reprinted arms. She saw their registration tattoos, *bio-equivalent* picked out in small red text. The tags were fake; the hack-job lifted her as if she were a child. The muscles had boosted strength at a minimum, maybe marrow batteries wired to alloy bones.

Alice's Marines training covered a range of interrogation scenarios. There was a point where the pain of torture overcame any training, so the aim was to prevent it from happening in the first place. There were two approaches—agree or disagree with the interrogator. First was to try to help from the start, stupidity replacing honesty: *Me? Oh no, sir, I didn't mean to, this is all a terrible mistake.* The other was to chew the scenery and fight back: *Get the hell away from me unless you want to end up hospital.*

This team of hack-jobs were grizzled and street worn. They must have heard every hard-luck story going, desperate people trying to sob their way through the market. Better to go out fighting.

Alice twisted and beat the thug's arm as hard as she could. It was like punching a steel plate.

"Hey numb nuts, put me down before we get ourselves a problem. I've errands to run." She windmilled her arms, struggling within his grip, her combat boots two feet from the floor. Laughter broke out as the guards enjoyed themselves.

"One-Eye, we got a complication. She triggered the prohibited-tech scan. Check her out." The hack-job holding her spoke with a light, effeminate voice that contrasted his overly pumped physique.

"Just let me go." Alice stopped struggling and went limp, a burst balloon.

The hack-job placed her delicately back on the deck and gave a mock bow.

"Thanks," Alice said. "Maybe you ain't a total ass after all."

The guard lifted a small plastic box with a text screen and whip antenna from his belt. It was home brew, hacked together from different parts, but its function was obvious enough. He waved it over the trash bag she was carrying. It beeped.

"Open up," he said.

Alice pulled out the Bunny Bopper to whistles of appreciation.

"Now what's a girl like you doing with proscribed tech like this?" The voice came from a normal-looking guy to the rear. Older, tall, silver hair. Cute in a movie-mobster kind of way.

"Good to see you're keeping the tradition of sexist jokes alive and well," Alice said. "Bet you like your girls all weak and simpering, huh? No room for stronger personalities in your world view."

The man stepped forward, ignoring everyone else, and the milling crowds drifted away. His left eye had been replaced by a metal pipe that protruded two inches and glowed with an inner red light. He was making a statement keeping it—new eyes only cost a few bucks.

"You must be One-Eye. What's the pipe for?" she said, nodding at his face.

"Helps me see the future."

"You carry it well."

"You're too kind. Now let's dispense with the pleasantries before I die of boredom. Bunny Boppers are illegal unless you are military or police. Where and how did you get it?"

"You're security on the Bridge and you're worried about illegal armaments?"

"Indulge me."

Alice had to be careful. This guy was charming, smooth and clever. If she started a long string of lies, he'd wrap them around her neck and strangle her. "Used to be a cop. Boosted it from the armory when they fired me."

One-Eye looked at her, unsmiling. "You're going to hang your life on that story?"

Alice tried to stay calm, but her arms and legs shook with tension, muscles stretched tight. Sweat ran across her back, her body itching to flee these predators. She closed her eyes and felt snow settle on her face, cold spots that melted and ran downward. Alice knew death's combination of denial and acceptance. She composed herself.

"Ain't no story, and I'm getting real tired of your approach."

"When did you graduate from the academy?"

"One year ago, first quarter."

"And you're military as well?"

"Marines. Domestic, then colonial."

"Precinct?"

"First, based at Canal across to west side."

"Go to Mars?"

"Yeah. Ask me about that and I'll kill you."

"Citations?"

"Thousands, same as any other cop. Got fired this morning for missing an HR presentation. I kept my jacket and raided the supply room before they kicked me out."

"Human resources are a time and resource suck," One-Eye replied, "but never ignore the rules."

"I was busy."

"You were stupid. Is the Bunny Bopper the only ordnance you're carrying?"

Fuck. If they search me and find my NYPD gear it's sayōnara, sister.

"Yes, I'm clean."

"While I appreciate your entirely plausible honesty, do you mind if we look for ourselves?" He didn't wait for an answer, turned to the hack-job who had grabbed Alice before. "Kika, do the honors."

Kika nodded to Alice, then held out his hand out as if asking for a dance. Alice took it with her left. She was right-handed, and had enough clearance to get a good one to his chin. Whether or not he had a glass jaw was out of her control. Kika took a silver beetle from his belt and placed it on her palm. It shook itself and she felt a faint tickling as it scuttled along her wrist and onto her jacket.

McNulty's Military Emporium stated their arachno-weave suits were a black hole to infrared and radar. Alice had purchased an extra stealth package guaranteed to hide her weapons from detection; if it was false advertising she wouldn't be around to claim a refund. The beetle chirped as it crawled over her, small green text scrolling across its back. It reached her ankles and gave a series of disappointed beeps.

"Search her," One-Eye said.

Alice pushed Kika away and unzipped her jacket's integrated backpack. Ten guns were on her in a blur, fat capacitors whining.

"Okay children, let's up the IQ and lower the testosterone." Alice gestured to her open jacket. "May I?"

One-Eye nodded. Alice pulled out her riot gun, the cheap plastic making it seem like a toy in her hands, and tossed it over. One-Eye caught it, flipped it around, pulled out the battery, and threw it back.

"That it?" he said.

"Didn't have time to tool up, what with losing my job."

"I heard Mars was bad."

Careful. "Yeah, it was the King Kong of fuck-ups."

"My brother died at Hellas Planitia."

"I was in the third Parliament run."

Kika whistled appreciatively behind her. Some bad news stuck with you forever.

"Then you are a true survivor." One-Eye gave a curt nod. "Armament sales are to the market's rear, near the first masonry tower. Your battery will be available upon departure."

"Get your number?" Alice asked as she put the Bunny Bopper away.

"I like my girls weak and simpering, remember?" He jerked his thumb toward the Bridge entrance. "Get moving."

As One-Eye turned from her, Kika made a writing motion with his hand. "Want mine?"

She didn't bother to reply, just stepped into the crowd and let herself be washed forward.

———

ALICE DID her best not to appear a tourist, but she hadn't seen anything like the market in years. Her diet as a runner consisted of little more than vat-grown rice and reprinted meat, which was a tasteless red paste. Food in the Marines was equally limited, but it at least had textures and flavors of its own. As a cop, she'd had to rely on her meager NYPD salary to survive. After rent and alcohol there wasn't much left for luxury items such as real food, so she lived off the same cheap sludge as when she was a kid.

Her current surroundings were so rich and substantial as to make her dizzy. There were fruit and vegetables everywhere, and the scent of damp soil hung heavy in the air. One vendor sold nothing but oranges. She couldn't stop herself from staring at their wet spheres, water glinting like diamonds.

She moved on, distracted, the mission, and its stakes,

momentarily forgotten. Her stomach cramped at the smell of sizzling onions on a hot plate. The next stall displayed an array of smoked meats and sausages hung like decorations. Alice had never seen real meat before: it was so bloody and raw she didn't know whether to throw up or beg to try it.

"Sample?" The man behind the counter smiled and held out a toothpick with a thin red disk on the end. Flavors she'd never imagined filled her mouth—fatty, spicy richness. She closed her eyes, body absorbing the juices.

"Good, huh?" The vendor nodded to the hanging meats around him. "Don't wanna rush, but I ain't got all day. Need to get water before curfew."

"Curfew?"

He looked at her, long and cool. "First time on the Bridge, huh?"

"That obvious?"

"Got nothing against greens, but not everyone's so gentle. Security, for instance, don't have no love for visitors. You need to get a rule list, and learn it fast. Curfew is at sundown—that's six. You're still a pedestrian in the Fourth Ward after that, things will turn bad."

"What sort of bad?"

"Look around ya." He waved in a circle, then motioned for the next customer.

Alice stepped back and took in her surroundings. Distracted by the sights, she hadn't been paying attention to the big picture: another rookie mistake. Stalls ran in both directions, some metal, some wood, some just kids sitting on barrels, selling cigarettes. The crowd was better fed than she was used to, but there was a growing tension in people's movements, the hurried certainty of limited time to complete essential tasks. Alice looked at the meat shack. The teller was staring at her, an expression on his face that she couldn't read.

She raised her head.

The Bridge's thick suspension cables cut graceful arcs between the twin stone towers, thinner steel rods dropping to the road edges. Between every third vertical rod, a body hung from a noose, feet swaying in the wind. There were ten, twenty, a hundred; each with a glowing sign tied around their neck outlining their crimes:

Food Hoarder.
Hid Income From Tax Inspector.
Refused To Share Apartment With New Families.
Broke Curfew.

The list went on and on. Alice saw now why the crowd was so quiet and polite, why they wouldn't hold eye contact for more than a second. Everyone was terrified. Fourth Ward wasn't an oasis in the wreckage of New York's streets, or a haven for citizens looking to provide for their families. It was a feudal dictatorship, its laws enforced with the most severe of penalties. Alice understood why people lived here—hot food and clean water cost a fortune these days—but the Bridge was nothing more than a slaughterhouse garlanded with flowers.

And Mike was in here somewhere.

Enough. It was time to find the evidence needed to call in SWAT, and get the hell away from this charnel house. Alice whispered into her collar, "Suit, any signs of Mike's tracker?"

"Oh, I'm allowed to talk now, am I?"

"I die in here, think you'll get handed over to lost property?"

"I concede your point. No, I have not detected Officer Squire's subcutaneous beacon yet."

"Mapping?"

"I could try to access the indigenous aerostat community, but I'm concerned that would mark me out as a police system."

"Okay. Shut up and let me concentrate."

"And there's the Officer Yu I love so much."

Alice pulled her collar up and pushed into the crowd.

One-Eye watched the stealth aerostat's video feed with a dry interest. The woman was lying, that much was obvious. He could have interrogated her at the entrance, found the real reason for her visit, but he'd learned to his cost that truths elicited by pain proved unreliable. Better to follow, find out what she wanted by stealth, then kill her.

Today might provide some fun after all.

[6]

"If such experiments continue, the inevitable conclusion is a new breed of superhumans. Those creations, combined with the relentless logic of MIs, suggest there will be little need for baseline humans afterward."
Pentagon Report, "War in the Age of Sentient Machines," President of the United States, 2053

"If we don't bring more revenue in, then New York is fucked. That's why the bridges, that's why the deals, that's why I can't sleep at night."
New York Mayor Thornley, Mafia wiretap, New York, 2053

When Red started up the ladder the Bridge's deck had looked high, but within reach. Now that he was halfway there, the truth was clear: the reason Fourth Ward didn't guard this access point was that only an idiot would attempt the climb.

Each frozen-metal rung was an icy brand across his palm. The pain in his arms passed from fire to a wooden numbness, muscles shivering with fatigue. Only desperate determination kept him climbing two, five, ten stories to reach the Bridge railing.

The wind was cold and strong. It moaned as it pushed between the suspension cables, his wet jeans freezing against his flesh. His heavy boots became dumbbells as he hauled himself up and over to fall onto the wooden decking of the Bridge. He couldn't move, his body welded to the floor, as his lungs fought for every scrap of oxygen.

He raised his head to see the backs of two young women selling apples at a small stall. He dragged himself to a crouch and reached back to grab the ladder's top; it vibrated under his palm. His pursuers were following him up.

Red stood and limped to the stall. He recognized the girls from his market days, but didn't know their names, and had always been too shy to ask until now.

"Hey." He said it quietly, trying not to startle them.

The closest turned, frowned, then smiled at him.

"Hey Red, what you doing back here? Got goods?" Her voice was rough from too many cigarettes. One hung from her bottom lip and bobbed with every word.

"Not today. I need your help." Those words had the same effect as ever. Her face hardened, barriers rising. "You know the Bridge better than me and—"

"I just work here, Red, okay? Gets the food, sells the food, is all I do. I don't know anyone with money, and I ain't got none either. You're a good kid. I just can't have any trouble, got enough of my own."

"I need a way through, you know, to the island?"

"Fuck you want to go there for?"

"Delivery." Red cursed inwardly. *Idiot*. "On the other side, I mean. Got a pick up."

"Uh-huh. I believe you." Her face told a different story.

"How do I get through?" He tried to stop desperation leeching into his voice, failed.

She seized on his weakness in a second. "Money." She held her hand out. "Nothing's ever for free."

"I will come back tomorrow, pay you double, okay?"

"Yeah, sure, you look trustworthy. Want my fruit as well? Maybe come by later and take my shoes?"

There was a shout from below. His pursuers were closer than he had thought. "Please, help me, *please*." He watched her consider, soften, attitude flipping.

"Okays, this once only, right? You ever want to sell on the Bridge again, you need to pay me five, no delays."

"Sure, deal, you got it." *Hurry, please hurry.*

"You can't get through at deck level, Fourth Ward have the center all closed off. Last I heard, crossing the cables was the only way. You climb the wire over there." She turned and pointed toward Manhattan. "There are people that live on 'em, high up, but they don't have Ward backing, as far as I know. Maybes you can negotiate with them, get a way through."

Red stepped forward and hugged her warm body, smelling cigarettes and dirt.

After a moment she pushed him away. "You owe me, understand? I know where you hang, Red. Don't forget this when I come calling."

Red didn't answer, just nodded and pushed past the fruit stall and zigzagged through the crowd as best he could.

His legs and feet were cold and stiff, ankle sore, but it warmed as he moved. He took breaths of the chill air in whooping lungfuls, exhaled clouds of white smoke as he kept moving. He thought about shouting at people to clear the way, but didn't want his pursuers to hear him. Could he lose them in the crowd? No chance—he was tall and his red hair stuck up in spikes. Looked awesome, but not so discreet.

He made his way toward the suspension cables. The crowd

emitted a hushed burble of voices, eyes down, everyone too aware of the approaching curfew to relax. Then shouts came from behind. Red fought his way forward, the need for stealth gone. He yelled and kicked, used his elbows and hands to force a way though. The cable entrance—a six-foot-tall steel box with a line of sharp points running across the top—grew before him.

With one last lunge, Red pushed through a tight knot of people to reach the base. The main suspension cable was thicker than his chest, and made from hundreds of smaller cables wound together. Every ten feet a thick node connected to a vertical cable holding up the deck. The remnants of a handrail system hung in pieces—now there was nothing but the cable rising into the storm.

Red gripped the top railing, palms between the steel points, and hauled himself up. His descent on the other side was less coordinated, and he fell spread-eagled onto the main cable. A thin layer of ice coated its surface, making it near impossible to grip. He shuffled himself around and half sat on, half hugged, the line of steel. He tried to inch forward, but it was like climbing a popsicle. Every few feet he would slide back to his starting point. His hands hurt from his ascent of the ladder and he could find no footholds.

For a moment the clouds cleared overhead, the storm blowing itself out, and he saw the full length of the cable. At the top, where it connected to the masonry tower, a bright red box with slit windows was glued to the stone wall. A long white pole lay horizontally across the cable blocking it, and a flickering neon sign spelled out *No Entry*. Even if he made it all the way up, there would be a crew waiting for him.

Forget it. He'd go the low road, try to sneak though.

He swung himself around to find the Crazy Horse kids less than twenty feet away, lips pulled back in toothy snarls. The sight of them made Red jump, his body shivering with fear.

"Gonna kill you, kill you," the nearest kid said.

Out of options, Red turned back to the icy cable and inched his way toward the clouds.

[7]

"Concerns such as yours are shortsighted; these machines are not to be feared like wolves in the dark. Yes, the potential for widespread societal change is present, just as it was for the wheel and printing press. Do not be scared. History will show this as another inflection point for mankind, one weighted toward positive outcomes."
Charles Takamatsu, CEO of Cortex, introducing the first 'Post-Turing' Mechanical Intelligence to the United Nations General Assembly, New York, 2044

"A Type 3 Mind is designed to be annoying, otherwise why pay attention to it? Within six hours of being worn, the NYPD smart jacket will produce a personality to counter the wearer's. The idea being that an antagonistic partner is more likely to keep the owner alert during a twelve-hour shift."
Jon Bonero, McNulty Military Apparel, unveiling the new NYPD street uniform to a less than appreciative academy class, 2050

Alice headed for the first tower and its weapons dealerships. The press of people, the swirling blurs of colors, the garbled conversations, triggered her Marines training and an icy calm fell over her. As she walked, she watched. How many security teams worked the market? What were their routes and schedules?

The further she went, the more the stalls and crowd changed. The food market, with its mob of scruffy unemployed, was at the Bridge's entrance. Next came hardware and tools: blowtorches, paint, ladders. Onward, the surroundings became more industrial. One stall had a broken analytical engine on display, the cracked brass sheet locked inside an armor-glass container guarded by a buzzing aerostat. The small ship's mylar body reflected its environs as it hovered, its needle weapon aimed at any shopper who wandered too close.

Then, at the rear, she reached weapons.

These stalls bore as much resemblance to the previous ones as a nuclear sub did to a rowing boat, being part Virt-Hub, part firing range. A cute guy with red hair and garish skater clothes smiled from a lounge chair before placing Virt nodes on his temples. It made sense; this way he'd get all the thrills of MDK—murder, death, kill—without having to shoot live munitions in a crowd zone. Half of New York's button men were here, buying the latest toys to kill cops.

Alice had to call Dispatch, yet she hesitated; was this enough to justify backup? Or would Central Dispatch fire her on the spot for being so far out of bounds? Her hand rested on her suit's collar stud, ready to make the call, but then she dropped it to her side again.

It wasn't worth the risk.

Yet.

She moved further along. Behind the stalls rose a twenty-foot-high wall of crushed cars topped with a line of remote guns and a satellite uplink array. A ten-foot-wide circular duct capped with ventilation grilles and a locked door projected from its center. A cheery neon sign read *Unauthorized Entry Will Be Met With Lethal*

Force in bright pink. Beyond the wall, Alice spotted Pentagon habitation units, their interlocking cardboard walls forming recognizable offices, dining halls and training rooms. Above that, fading into the falling snow, were hints of glass and steel geometries.

Alice paused, unsure what to do next, as the deep *thwack* of a helicopter grew to buffet the crowd. She'd not seen a mechanical aircraft in years, and she squinted as a downdraft blew dust and dirt into her face. The large vehicle settled on a landing pad glued to an upper level platform. The machine looked old and repurposed, encrusted with weapons and comms gear. The Bridge rattled beneath it. The rotor's vibration shook her feet, then the noise cut off.

"You a smoker, yeah?" a voice said.

Alice turned to see a slim boy dressed in a huge, threadbare fur coat. A knitted pom-pom hat was pulled over most of his face, with only his jug ears protruding.

"How could you tell?" She shivered as cold seeped through her clothing, the stimulant inhaler fading.

"You're thin, got a hungry look, yet you're scoping out the weapon shacks. You've enough cash to buy the latest toys, but not for food. That's a vice or two right there."

Alice laughed. "You got me. What you selling?"

"Twelve for five Obamas, singles for a Gipper."

"Give me a single."

Alice handed over the plastic note. The kid reached into a deep pocket and gave her a white tube. She flicked the toggle and sucked in the bitter smoke, let her bruised ribs protest as she exhaled a cloud of carcinogens. "Been here all day?"

"Sunrise to sunset."

"Seen anything unusual?"

His expression was clear enough. *Unusual? Here?* He shrugged.

"Let me be more specific," Alice said. "A friend of mine was jacked. Think he came through here. You see that?"

He shrugged again. "Seen a lot of things, maybe."

Alice sighed, zipped open a thigh pocket and pulled out a wad of old notes. "Ten Gippers. All I've got. This help?"

The kid reached out; Alice raised the notes out of his reach.

"Yeah, yeah, I get it, no need for theatrics." He nodded at the money. "You better give that, though. None of this getting intel then zipping them away, right? I got friends here. You'll never make it back to civilian turf, you do me wrong. Okay?"

"Talk, Einstein. I'm on a schedule."

"So, yeah, a big-boy catch team came through maybes an hour ago, right? They had this poor dude all wrapped up in plastic. No respect for the little guy, those teams—knocked over my dad's stall on the way. Hate 'em, but what you gonna do? That's why I always sells personal. No stall for me, all goods are in my pockets, easy to avoid conflict and stuff if you go one-on-one."

Alice held her frustration at bay. She lowered the money. "How many of them?"

"Two guys. One carrying, one clearing the way."

"You willing to put that on the record, let me vid you saying it? I'd come back with more money later, make your day." An eyewitness was one of Central Dispatch's requirements to hit ninety percent probability and justify the expense of a SWAT rescue team.

The kid backed away from her, a look of disgust on his face. "You a Scorcher?"

"In a previous life."

"You're on Ward territory. You that stupid?"

She took a pull on the cigarette, blew out another cloud. *Figured it couldn't be that easy.* "Just tell me where they went and we're good."

"Through there." He pointed at the ventilation duct. The one with the cheery *Lethal Force* sign.

"Well, there's a surprise." Alice said and finished her smoke as the sun set behind her.

Alice looked through the grille. The duct doubled as a corridor; someone had welded a flat metal plate across the curve to form a basic floor. She tilted her head and listened. Faint echoes and shouts came from within, but nothing that hinted where the duct lead. A strong breeze sucked her forward and she had to hold her hair back with one hand. The grille and door were heavy steel mesh tied together by a rotary lock.

She had tools in her jacket that could open this in seconds, but she needed time to think, so she walked to the Bridge edge and looked down. There was a commotion around one of the fish holes cut into the ice and a small group chasing someone.

Manhattan glittered to her left, towers piercing the uplit sky. Through a gap in the storm clouds she saw thousands of automated craft streak back and forth in a mix of red and white navigation lights. Crystal droplets glistened on the towers' upper skins, the faintest hint of blue and green under the dying sun. Alice had heard rumors of sprawling forests under geodesic domes, of seas trapped inside mile-wide glass bubbles, of rosewood boulevards filled with laughter. Each tower had its own internal security, so the chance she'd ever see for herself was remote.

She sighed and looked down at her hands. Why was she hesitating? Her plan was still valid: get the evidence she needed, then contact Central Dispatch while she escaped.

Because she was scared, that was why. Scared of the tunnels.

The dark edges of claustrophobia crowded her vision, the first tendrils of a panic attack that would trap her here. She could fool everyone except herself—Mars was still with her, inside, festering. Mars: it always came back to that hateful planet, everything did.

MARTIAN INDEPENDENT REPUBLIC, 2052

The drop ship *It's Been A Long Week* fell from the *Fucker* like a lead brick. The descent was smooth at first, there being no atmosphere to kick it around, so Alice rechecked her gear. Eight straps tied her into the ejection seat, and the emergency-launch wire bobbed over her right shoulder. The seat was a smart composite that remolded itself to balance loads. She hated it, the crawling sensation was too much like being groped by an old man.

Her gun clipped to a tactical sling across her body armor. It was pre–machine phase and heavy. There were nineteen other Marines in the containment vessel, and everyone thought Alice was an idiot for lugging such a weapon around. She looked at them now, each equipped with a standard-issue plastic centrifuge gun. They were lightweight, battery powered, and maintenance free. Alice had fought long and hard to use her own gear, but it was worth it. While her platoon would be hosing people down with tiny aluminum pellets, she could put a fist-sized hole through someone at a thousand yards. No one would be getting up and filing an HR complaint after that.

"Mission feed active," a digital voice whispered inside her helmet.

Alice pulled a thin pair of yellow visors from a pocket and slipped them on, strapping her helmet again afterward. At first the feed was blackness. She guessed it was space, but no, it was just the log-in process. Then Mars was there, below her in such clarity that vertigo said hello. For a moment she thought she'd puke, but her training took over and she settled in, looking for details. Her drop ship was the middle of the three from the *Fucker*. The *Why Can't We Just Get Along?* led the way, and would coordinate with the spec-ops team to blow the domes' central hexagon. Her ship would land and secure the Parliament's external circulation ring, while the *Sorry For The Mess* would take on Parliament itself. It had the glamorous job of breaking the sun dome and setting down in the midst of the debate chamber.

The UN envoy and her bodyguards were dead, of course. Alice still couldn't figure why the Moles had done that. They had been logical in their demands until then. Unreasonable, yes, deluded, certainly, but they hadn't crossed the line into crazy town. Even after their bootstrapped systems had slaughtered the first two waves of Marines, their requests had been clear enough: recognition of Mars as an independent colony, and ownership rights to the land they had already colonized. The UN agreed to open talks after those early military debacles, hence the envoy offering to speak at the Martian Parliament. That's when it had all gone wrong. The Moles butchering the UN team on live TV, and sending the Virt worldwide.

There was no room for negotiations after that. The *Fucker* was not a warship, but it carried an orbital missile launcher fastened between its foil radiators. In the hours following the broadcast the ship blew two domes without warning, assault teams occupying the surrounding tunnels looking for survivors.

There hadn't been any.

And now the Marines were going in. Both sides had limited resources and personnel. No one knew of the Moles' exact numbers, but it was thought to be under four hundred. Two hundred Marines had traveled up from Earth, taking four-hour shifts wedged into bunks deemed too small for use even on submarines. The confines reminded Alice of the sewers back home, where she and Paulie had hidden that first brutal winter.

Military doctrine assumed the Moles would be cowed scientists armed with pitchforks and sharp sticks. Instead, they faced people who had switched planets in the search for a new life. People who were hard, smart, and desperate. But one way or the other, this would be over today. If the drop failed, the *Fucker* would nuke the structure from orbit, let fires cleanse the site for the next round of settlers.

The first edges of atmosphere shook the drop ship. Subtle at first, then harder, until Alice gripped the arms of her ejection seat, knuckles white, equipment clattering around her. Mars swelled below her, the thin air coating the ship's camera with red dust.

The *Fucker*'s Mechanical Intelligence controlled their flight path. Alice watched the *Why Can't We Just Get Along?* flatten out of its descent arc, the deep blue of its drive clipped from view. The Parliament dome grew ahead, a tiny white dot at first, then its structure became clear. Delicate trusses held fifty-foot-wide hexagonal pillows in place, their translucent plastic leeching radiation from the sunlight.

"We are green on all channels, execution in five ... four ..." Alice's helmet said.

She sucked in air and blew it between her teeth. This was it. After all the training, all the drills, the long journey up here, they were going in. Another wave of turbulence shook the craft, and adrenaline sizzled through her. The air was cold, but sweat ran between her shoulders and her shaved scalp prickled.

Calm it girl, do your job.

"... three ... two ... one ... ignition."

The *It's Been A Long Week* had two planar drives to its rear. Their shielding was over a foot thick, but the *boom* of activation rattled the whole ship. They accelerated, and a hand squashed her chest until she was gasping for breath.

Through her visors she watched the lead drop ship arrow down toward the dome. For a moment it appeared it would crash into the structure, then the central hex-panel glowed with blue-white fire and split apart. The *Why Can't We Just Get Along?* powered through. Alice's ship followed, increasing in velocity as it approached. As it shot past the opening, Alice glimpsed the spec-ops team that had climbed up to lay the demolition charges.

This dome contained the Moles' main source of water and vegetation. The Parliament building comprised a lightweight metal roof capping an existing crater, the interior hollowed out to accommodate a pulpit and seating. A thirty-foot-wide boulevard of concrete encircled its exterior, in turn surrounded by a moat of fresh water. Only two feet deep, it glittered tropical blue under the dome lights. A stunted forest of modified fir trees filled the remaining space, with small circular playgrounds at each hour mark.

White phosphorous sprayed from the underside of the lead ship, and Alice watched it fall onto the forest, the dry woods bursting into flames. Another *boom* flung her against her straps, the aircraft engaging a hard-brake maneuver. Her visors slid down her nose so she lost the view, but for a moment she saw people running from the fires.

People on fire.

People only a few feet tall.

Then everything went black. Not nighttime dark, not countryside dark, but the absolute nothingness of an underground cave. The craft shook so violently that Alice's visors flew away from her head, while her arms and legs lost contact with the chair and floor. Her stomach flipped as the ship rolled onto its back and plummeted, a dead weight. The buffeting grew until she saw stars, unable to breathe, g-force crushing her chest. People screamed around her.

"Marines, use your zip cords *now*," Top, forever calm, shouted amidst the deafening racket.

Alice reached up and behind her for the emergency launch wire, but in the dark, her body spinning with the craft's tumbling roll, she couldn't find it. She tried again. How long had they been falling? She had no idea; the ground must be seconds away at best. The spin continued, shaking so violently that Alice didn't know what was up or down. She grasped behind her, desperate, the seat's hard edges under her fingers, the weight of her helmet crushing. She traced left along its edge, blood filling her mouth. She screamed in fear, found the cable, and pulled hard.

For a moment she thought it hadn't worked—the leash came away in her hand—then it clicked and her seatbelts pulled agonizingly tight. There was a shuddering *rat-tat-tat* and something was in her mouth, bitter and dry, filling her up, swelling and hardening as it reached her lungs. A second of devastating inertia and she—

———

NEW YORK, 2055

Alice screwed her eyes shut, forced the memories away, and turned from the view of a frigid Manhattan. She unsheathed the riot gun, hung it on her tactical sling, and pulled a new battery pack from a thigh pocket. It clicked home with a low-pitched buzz as the cartridges accelerated. She took a small silver key from another pocket. In one smooth movement she crossed to the metal mesh door, inserted the smart key until it pulsed, then dragged it open and ducked inside.

The half-inch-long mylar teardrop of One-Eye's aerostat waited ten seconds, then followed her.

[8]

"With this new reprinting technology, the entire medical profession, from the humble pharmacist to the most skilled surgeon, has become irrelevant overnight. Those able to afford these treatments could, in theory, live forever."
Sarah Spencer, CEO of Hymann Reprint Boutiques Inc., Los Angeles, 2047

―――

"Van Gogh obsessed over sunflowers because they are the lion of the flower world. Tall, beautiful, fleeting; Cortex surgical systems are proud to use them as a logo."
Patsy Conroy GS, unveiling Cortex's MI remote surgical systems, New York, 2049

―――

PATSY CONROY, AKA PIGGY BANK, AKA THAT'S MR. BANK TO You, dug into the greenhouse's rich brown soil with a ceramic trowel.

Its vibrating blade curled a small plug from the damp earth. He withdrew a single white seed from his belt, then placed it with the utmost care at the bottom of the new hole.

Conroy had seen the revolution coming. Unable to alter history, he'd sidestepped humanity's downfall to take a seat on the sidelines. After mankind's millennium at the apex, he watched it be replaced over ten years of MI rollout.

Creating a new life had been more challenging than expected, however, the ingrained patterns of the past requiring determination to overcome. He shouldn't have been surprised; after twenty years as a surgeon, the last five with a certain notoriety, he had an abundance of personality to reprogram.

He reached into a nearby plastic bucket for a bolus of black soil, and inhaled the odor of peat with contentment. Conroy had sent a security team far north for this sod, a journey with costs that far outweighed the return. His assistants had told him the mission was a bad idea, a waste of resources. They were wrong, but Conroy didn't blame them for such naivety. Like many of his young family, they lived day to day and knew nothing of world building. Conroy had survived and flourished because he understood the value of a brand, and built his with care.

Take his street name, for example: Piggy Bank. A long dead rival had meant it as a slur, suggesting that Conroy was the epitome of filth and greed. Conroy saw it another way. A pig would eat its own shit to survive, while banks were instruments of *power*. Power used to come from money; now it came from family.

He squeezed the fresh soil into a fat sausage, curled it around the white seed, and filled in the hole. His family hadn't understood the long trip north, and didn't understand his obsession with sunflowers, a symbol that permeated the Fourth Ward's kingdom.

He had known of their doubts, and explained his actions this one time. Sunflowers, fleeting yellow bursts, were in themselves less than worthless; they were a resource suck. So why his obsession? For beauty, that was why. Any family rich enough to sponsor the arts was a family to be feared. Fourth Ward was his alone, the merest hint of dissent quashed. Now it was time to make it beautiful.

He wasn't greedy, had no need to be a One, had no desire to leave the streets and retire to the pearlescent corridors of the sky. The one percent hadn't changed with the automation tsunami, and so continued as if nothing had happened. They clucked quiet disapproval as their heads were laid upon the chopping block, mistook the executioner's blade for stars in the sky.

Conroy didn't need to climb the towers. If he waited long enough, they would fall at his feet.

His back popped as he stood, took a step forward, and settled on his haunches again. He liked the smell in here: so human, so organic. The new world reeked of hot brass and coolants, of plastic flesh and acid sealants. It was no longer fit for man, machinery now the apex predator.

He planted a new seed.

Fertilized it.

Stood.

Once upon he'd been a surgeon, a job with a definition that changed as fast as the super-heated weather systems. A scalpel wielder at first, saving lives, then saving faces. Next, a military consultant, and, finally, a delivery boy for intelligent machines.

Most of his colleagues took an old-fashioned view of technology, thought their blade skills were irreplaceable. Arrogance masked fear of the new, and Conroy had found himself ostracized when he partnered with the first licensed MI surgeon. Organic reprinting had transformed surgery into a task befitting a car mechanic: find the broken part and replace it. So when Cortex approached him to field test their new machines he'd agreed without hesitation.

He had expected to miss the blood, the smell, the power of the operating theater. He didn't. At first, he supervised the MI from within the same room, then from an adjacent one, and finally from his office, via an array of Virt screens.

His sojourn at the Pentagon offered a short-term break in routine.

Reprinting Martian soldiers from the safety of Manhattan was an interesting challenge, but with time his job dwindled to supervising Mechanical Intelligences for legal reasons, and once the law was repealed, there was nothing at all for him to do.

He'd checked out long before that, of course, had spotted the increased reliance of the poor upon each other and begun the metamorphosis into Mr. Bank.

Tribalism would return when a population could no longer look after its own. The strong and tightly bound families would prevail. Organized crime had been defeated when he was a student, but its lessons were universal and he was a quick study. After that final day of employment, he liquidated his assets and set out to turn the poorest and most-abused members of society into a new family.

Take One-Eye, who now approached him. His eye, a low-grade neuro-ophthalmic sensor, was a symbol of his upbringing and he wore it with pride. That eye was his sunflower; he kept it as part of his personal branding.

Lights blossomed as Conroy rose, industrial warehouse units glowing with the wide spectrum illumination perfect for plant life.

Seventy-six plantings. Not bad for a middle-aged man with an injured back. He looked around at the two thousand sunflowers glowing gold. Perfect.

"Yes?" he said when One-Eye reached him.

"Your call is in an hour."

"Is the shipment on schedule?"

"Yes sir."

"And?"

"We have an unusual problem."

"Of course we do."

One-Eye had been with Conroy from the beginning. The heat of the greenhouse brought that day back into sharp focus—the glaring marble walls of the lobby, the fat security guard and hated HR woman smiling from behind the barrier, the half-blind boy outside the Rockefeller Center's FEMA tent, too weak to stand.

"Show me," Conroy said, and stepped away from his flowers.

ONE-EYE LED Conroy through a series of hot, cramped metal corridors. The Bridge creaked around them, the storm-force winds loading its cables to their limits. After five minutes they entered the security surveillance room.

Many things had changed with the advent of Mechanical Intelligences, yet many tasks remained the same. The room was on the cusp of this dilemma. Advanced smart-systems tracked every person on the Bridge. Those systems suggested people of interest who were then followed by human teams or dedicated aerostats. It would have been easier, and more efficient, to automate security, but Conroy was old school and trusted human intuition more than data sets.

The room was circular, the boss chair raised in the middle surrounded by operators, their screens available at a glance from the center seat. The lighting was dim, only the blue-white monitors illuminating thin faces. What little chatter there was faded as Conroy entered and took the central chair, One-Eye at his shoulder.

"Who is this?"

The video feed came from an aerostat's camera. The tunnel was dimly lit by red lights, the large screen flickering with more noise than usual. Still, the detail was good enough. A tall, athletic-looking Japanese woman in black stealth gear moved along a circular corridor. Her heart-shaped face was covered with dirt and sweat, while long black hair was tied back in a severe knot. She wore a police-grade visor and carried a riot gun tucked into her shoulder. The way she moved, with small, quiet steps, suggested military training.

Conroy's right foot, a long, curved piece of composite, ached in the damp. Like One-Eye's sensor, he kept it as a reminder to take nothing for granted, not even warm shoes on a cold morning.

"All information post her foster-home files are federally

encrypted," One-Eye said. He handed Conroy a tablet. "We've run every search we can, nothing."

"So she's a cop or military?"

"That's the working hypothesis. The sooner our source provides a back door into the Federal MI network, the better."

"Don't get comfortable with these toys," Conroy said. "Have faith in yourself. Your instincts have proven a valuable asset over the years. Take this woman, for example. You wouldn't have tagged her if she was authentic."

"We held her at security, but I didn't buy her answers. Said she was going to sell a Bunny Bopper in the arms sector."

"You saw it?"

"Yes sir."

"And you let her bring it *onto* the Bridge?" There was a tone to the question that chilled the room, the mumble of voices quieting.

"She seemed healthy, and well equipped," One-Eye said. "Not your usual pedestrian looking to buy drugs or food. If I sent her away, I believed she would return, and we could miss her the second time. I decided to let her through and tag her, find out what she wanted. I planned to pick her up as soon we knew. She is, however, proving more resourceful than expected."

"I think her target is obvious enough, don't you?" Conroy turned back to the screen.

"Officer Squire?"

"Did you read his capture report?"

"I apologize sir, I have not."

"You need to follow all the details, not just the headlines."

"Understood, sir. What did the reports say?"

"The team used a Thumper on his partner, per instructions." Conroy handed the tablet back to One-Eye. "I assumed the organic damage, plus job threat, would prevent the partner from following. It appears I was mistaken." He nodded at the screen. "What do you make of her?"

"She said she served in the Colonials on Mars. That would explain the tunnel combat training."

"So she's a Martian veteran now working for the NYPD?"

"Sir, I thought—"

"And you let her onto the Bridge carrying a Bunny Bopper; ordnance that if used correctly could topple this whole enterprise into the East River."

One-Eye didn't move. The room was silent and still apart from a security guard who drew his weapon, ready to kill Red-Eye if commanded.

"How is the current delivery schedule?" Conroy said.

"The last helicopter is here, the arms will be delivered ahead of schedule."

Conroy looked at the screen. He hated working with outside contractors, and the paranoia of using a helicopter made him wince. His family was a monument to a group ethic; live and die together. He rescued them, they saved him. As soon as outsiders contaminated the mix, his ability to control outcomes dropped. The truth, however, was that he couldn't do this alone.

He'd needed help to take over the Bridge; financial investments from certain venture-capital firms, and technical supplies from specific military suppliers. In return he had to manufacture products for his investors. Products so illegal it made drug trafficking look like selling candy. That deal was over today however, the last of the produce being loaded onto the waiting helicopter at this very moment. Once this final shipment had been delivered, a new arrangement would be in place. From tomorrow, every member of his family, from the lowest Bridge scraper, to the tip of the spear, would receive comprehensive healthcare. Such a simple thing, life, yet more persuasive than any drug.

Fourth Ward had the largest army in the five boroughs, and that brought strength through fear. Fear alone, though, wasn't enough to build loyalty. With this deal complete, everyone would know Fourth Ward was the family to join. *Work with us and you'll get the best healthcare in the modern world, while being protected by security systems designed by the Pentagon.* After that the other families would all fall in line. *If* he could deliver on his promises.

"Where is Officer Squire?"

"At the holding post on Peach," One-Eye said. Peach Street, the Bridge's nickname for its array of prison cells. "We can kill him now, drop the body in her path. She walks away, we made our point, job done."

"No. I've known Michael for seventeen years. I performed corrective surgery on his wife, donated money to charities he supported. He's been my man before this thing of ours, and yet he was willing to sell me—us—out and I want to know why his allegiances changed. Loyalty binds us together. That goes, so do we. Understand?"

"Yes sir. I'll send a kill team in straight away. She disappears on the Bridge, no way the NYPD can pin it on us."

"Do it fast, don't give her a chance," Conroy said. "Now, if that's your only point of failure today, I have a meeting to attend."

[9]

"Until you've met a Mechanical Intelligence, you can't fully comprehend how far behind we've fallen. The time is coming when we will have as much in common with them as they do ants."
"The Larson Paper" on rights due to Mechanical Intelligences, presented to UN delegates, 2040

"An unregulated MI is the deadliest opponent I can think of. There's a reason the Pentagon loves them so."
Sally Russoe, Smart Weapons Designer, Paris, TX, USA, 2050.

"It's rather nice isn't it? Not too large either. I bought it from a little gallery down on the fortieth floor. It used to belong to the Metropolitan Museum, and I didn't want it going to some tourist vacationing here. It was cheap, just a few million. Well, seventeen, but who's keeping track?"

Robin R. Lathamp III, Blade Tower 7 (AKA *The Molly Mansion*), Unit 7855, New York, 2052.

———

ALICE MOVED A FEW CORNERS AWAY FROM THE ENTRANCE AND then stopped. She kneeled and strapped the screen back onto her wrist, toggled the tracker system.

"Suit?"

"What?"

"Any signals?

"Of course not, I would have told you. There's a lot of interference down here which is proving difficult to see through. We should expect a messy signal until we get closer."

Alice put her cracked visors on, the yellow lenses sagging to the right. Their millimeter-wave radar mapped the tunnel's contours with a hard green edge, while the air glowed red, then purple, with shifting heat patterns. She considered using her drone; decided against it. Its battery was small and old, and she would need it to call Central Dispatch if she found the evidence.

A large duct repurposed from some ancient transport vessel appeared. A thick steel plate had been welded across to form a floor, while vertical seams spiraled around its surface every few feet. The force of air pushing past her was stronger here, the tunnel collecting and focusing the gale. Then it stopped. Alice staggered backward with the sudden lack of pressure. It returned warm, then hot, as if she were inside some slumbering animal.

Alice moved inward and the dim external light faded to a feeble silver flicker. A series of algae packs traced a haphazard line across the ceiling as they glowed a deep, aquatic green.

Water dripped, faint machine noises buzzed, but she heard no speech.

Alice now had a rough feel for the organization of the Bridge.

Most employees, or whatever they were, occupied the habitation layers above these tunnels. Down here she could avoid them while searching for Mike's tracker.

She splayed her feet against the wall, thirty degrees out from her body to form a stable tripod, then checked her riot gun. The front cartridge held plain aluminum rounds, the rear held a mix of steel and rubber-ceramic composite: ricochet bullets ideal for firing around corners, or using the curved walls of a tunnel to focus damage. Alice swapped the drums without looking, the actions learned from thousands of repetitions.

She was as ready as she could be, her body tight with tension, muscles hot. She forced herself to relax, took deep breaths, and concentrated on her training.

This ain't Mars, kid. Time to get it on.

THE TUNNEL CONTINUED STRAIGHT, then began a series of zigzags that were hard to navigate. The air was sultry, no cold in-breath anymore, just constant fetid gases carrying the stink of burning plastic and metal.

The skin on her back crawled at the thought of being trapped in here, alone.

"Suit?"

"Oh, for God's sake. Do you have any idea how annoying you are? *Suit, suit, suit, suit,* all the time. I have a perfect memory system you know: complete, total, pure recall. I remember everything you've ever said. Everything. There is no need to ask me again, *ever,* if I've located Officer Squire's tracker. Do you understand me? Never, *ever,* ask me again. Ever, ever, ever. If I get anything I'll tell you. Now shut up and let me concentrate."

Alice gave her jacket the finger and moved on.

The circumference of the duct decreased as she progressed, the steel walls closing around her. She crossed into an area that looked older, but made from higher-quality construction. The metal was of a heavier gauge, free from the buckling of the earlier sections, while the overheads changed from gel packs to emergency lights buried within wire cages.

An increasing amount of pipes and cables appeared—at first just a few multicolored wires, then thicker black tubes that sprouted to form roped bundles. Alice had seen system growth like this once before: the Marines ship, *Fuck You Looking At?* that took her to Mars.

President Harper made a big deal about the *Fucker*, as it came to be called, being the Colonial Marine's first system-capable warship. The grunts wedged inside knew what it really was—a repurposed NASA Jupiter Mission vessel. There was a clear logic to the design: habitation sphere at one end, nuclear drives at the other, separated by long lattice beam filled with fuel and supplies. To deal with the larger crew and new weapon suites, upgraded power cabling ran from the reactors to the front habitat. In true military fashion, there had been nothing beautiful about these additions, just black rubber conduits tracing the shortest route. Efficiency above all. It was the same on the Bridge; whoever built these systems had money but limited time. It took six more minutes of inching forward into the hot, damp tubes to find Mike.

"Positive track," Suit's voice buzzed from her collar speaker.

"Show me." Alice looked at her wrist screen. A three-dimensional diagram showed a vertical stack of walls, horizontal floors, and a flashing dot. "Distance?"

"Exact location parameters are difficult to ascertain. There is increasing interference both from denser bridge structures and the presence of heavy elements between us."

"What?"

"There appears to be a nuclear reactor somewhere in here."

"There's a reactor on the Bridge? Their power draw can't be that big."

"It is interesting—the cooling and ventilation capacity of these tunnels exceed that of all modern fusion reactors."

"So what's it for?"

"I'm a slaved smart-system; deductive leaps are best left to synthetic intelligences, or in desperate times, humans. If it's not too much trouble, may I suggest we concentrate on Officer Squire? Afterward, perhaps we can discuss energy densities and cooling requirements of modern machinery."

"Yeah, yeah." She studied the wrist map. "Okay, to get up to him we need—"

The submachine gun's roar was deafening in the confined space. Alice's hearing reduced to hissing white noise as gunfire thumped across the back of her jacket. She dived and scrabbled forward, checking for wounds. Her fragile luck held: the bullets hadn't triggered the Bunny Bopper. If that thing blew, they'd be scraping her from midtown facades.

She tore a concussion grenade from her belt and tossed it behind her, covering her ears as best she could. It exploded, sending searing bolts of lightning along the duct while the shock waves sent her skidding across the floor of the tunnel.

Choking black smoke filled the tube, the reek of burning metal overpowering. More gunfire strobed and whirred overhead as Alice rolled left and returned a long burst from the riot gun, its chainsaw bark like a tree being felled. She aimed upward at forty-five degrees so that the rounds scattered throughout the space. There were screams from behind, then muzzle flashes and more wasted rounds over her head.

The gang attacking her were enthusiastic and aggressive, but fought as if this were open-air combat, trying to hit her center mass. Alice had learned on Mars that using the tunnel walls to channel fire was a far more effective way to cause damage. She swept another round of ricochet bullets into the smoke, pushed herself up, and ran.

———

ALICE CHANGED DIRECTION AT RANDOM, zigzagging through tunnels and odd, open interconnections. After two minutes she stopped and listened for sounds of pursuit. Her ragged breath echoed from the curved walls as the discordant hisses and hums of machinery rumbled beneath her feet.

"A little help?" Alice said as she checked the riot gun's charge.

"My sensors are somewhat degraded by the Bridge's superstructure. I'd suggest you don't rely on me to find a way out."

"There's a surprise."

She heard shouts, faint at first, then growing in volume and joined by running footsteps. They knew where she was. Alice rounded a corner and sprinted flat out along the thirty-foot length of the connecting corridor, her desperate footfalls audible despite her damaged hearing. Her chest tightened, legs rubbery with fatigue. The junction at the end of the corridor gave her two options; left behind a closed wire door, or right and curving out of sight.

Gunfire opened up again. Hot, heavy impacts thudded across her jacket, and shrapnel whirred past to leave deep gouges in the metal walls. She kicked the door open, ran through, and unzipped a thigh pocket to pull out a smart claymore mine. Its six-inch body had two buttons on top: one for a trip wire, one for location sensitivity. She toggled the second and a small red LED glowed, indicating an active charge. Alice tore off the rear sticky pads, slapped the claymore onto the wall, then set off, head down, sprinting with every ounce of energy she had left.

How long had it been?

Three seconds?

Five?

The tunnel ran straight. The mine was loaded with rubber bearings designed for suppression control. If it triggered when she was in the blast radius, her jacket's bulletproof fabric would be as much use as a towel, the rounds knocking her unconscious at the very least.

At the junction ahead, soft red lighting illuminated a left and right split. As Alice reached it, a shock wave lifted her from the deck and dashed her back against the steel floor. The first explosion was echoed by a second, smaller but longer. The mine had ignited something else, maybe a power conduit. The noise was a physical force that shook her, vision flickering. Emergency lights flashed, flared, cut out. She'd lost her visors somewhere, and now the dark was absolute. Her lungs filled with choking black smoke, and she dry retched onto the cold metal floor.

Suit was talking, shouting, but she couldn't hear it. Her coughing was worse now; Alice hacked phlegm from deep inside, then vomited uncontrollably. She rolled onto her back, the riot gun still clipped to her chest, and struggled to read her wrist pad through the smoke. Green text scrolled across its small screen.

>: *Hello? Alice? Hello? Do you hear me?*

"Yeah," she mouthed, but couldn't hear herself. The floor of the tunnel shook beneath her, the tertiary explosions lost in her damaged hearing.

>: *Using a claymore in here was stupid, hear me? Stupid. We're on a stealth mission, not some commando raid.*

"Think we're a bit beyond that, don't you?" Alice said. The smoke was thicker; a warm, heavy texture that forced its way between her lips and into her mouth. "Now would be a really good time for some options though." She gave a deep, wracking cough.

>: *That's what I've been trying to tell you. The walls of this duct are significantly colder than previously, and the air exchange rate has risen enough to suggest—*

Alice twisted and raised the riot gun to shoulder height, firing a sustained burst at the side wall. The thin galvanized steel shredded into a cloud of confetti and she winced as a bitter, cold wind blew inward. The smoke cleared to reveal ragged rooftops of repurposed military housing modules huddled below a web of bird-catcher nets. She watched a diving gull become entangled in the netting's thick, sticky folds. It struggled, only to wrap itself in deeper.

A vine of cabling ran vertically past the houses, tied to a steel lattice, then arced upward to a conduit near her head. She reached up and out to grab the nearest cable. It was thin and yellow, the outer rubberized layer glittered with a hexagonal pattern: diamond thread fibers, more military tech. It seemed Fourth Ward had hooked itself deep into the Pentagon's supply chain. A cord this thick could leash a helicopter.

Alice's gloves were tough, made from the same fabric as her suit, but this would hurt. She gripped the cable with both hands, then swung out over the drop. There was a sickening moment of vertigo as the dark and hot confines of the tunnel were replaced with cold and white nothing. She wrapped her legs around the line and loosened her grip. Slow at first, then faster, she slid downward. There were shouts, and bullets tracked her from the duct—only a few rounds at first, but as alarms rang out, additional crackling gunfire came from the buildings below. She gathered speed, the wind a roar in her ears, as Fourth Ward staff scurried onto the uneven rooftops. She was lucky none of them had any real training, their guns a mixture of family heirlooms whose rounds fell beneath her, or more modern gear that required proper training.

Alice clung to the cable, arms and legs shaking with exertion, wind roar matched by the ripping hiss of the wire against her suit. Friction heat seared a line across her body, her hands agony. No matter what was below, her grip would fail in a few seconds.

The shanty town became a blur; tracer rounds fizzed past her head. A flat, snow-covered roof approached as her vision wavered, the bitter air making her squint.

"Suit, give me a solution," she shouted into the wind.

It buzzed back at her, voice whipped away.

"*What?*" she screamed.

"Now, now, now," Suit shouted, the collar speaker blowing in a small shower of sparks that sizzled against her neck.

Alice let go, and the burning brand across her hands extinguished in an instant. She tried to roll, execute a parachute landing, but her sideways momentum was too great and she smacked down on the roof's tough membrane, skidding like a hockey puck. She came up in a crouch, riot gun jammed to her shoulder, then flicked the rapid fire toggle only to see both cartridges had melted. She slid the tactical sling over her head and tossed it. Gunfire continued to track her, so she sprinted across the roof. Without looking, she put her foot on the edge and leaped across to the next roof. Down with a *bang*, the shock bone deep, then up and moving again. Breath harsh and heavy, oxygen-limited muscles begging for relief.

Shouts from behind, more gunfire kicking up snow at her feet and spattering against her jacket. Lower caliber than the tunnel's kill team; maybe farmers with guns used to scare birds away from their crops.

Alice needed cover before someone with a homemade bottle rocket blew her legs off. She looked up to see a dull orange sunset peek beneath the clouds. She was nearing the Bridge's perimeter; this line of military prefabricated units connected to another series a story below. She skidded onto her side, slid to the edge, then held onto a cheap metal gutter filled with blackened water. Ten feet down, another series of office modules ran parallel toward an alley one block over. She dropped, scuttled across, and fell into the tight space.

She knew it was a mistake the moment she landed. The alley was narrow and barely lit by the setting sun. Stagnant sea water and rotting vegetables fouled the air. These were older prefab units, covered with military stamps from the Pentagon's latest little wars: Canada, Mexico, and more than most, Mars. Alice tried to move forward, but the space was so cramped she had to turn sideways after a few feet. The wet floor and fibrous cables tripped and snagged her every movement.

She elbowed her way to the end and staggered out onto a small town square where a three-man security team was waiting for her. The second she cleared the alleyway, they raised their guns, each sporting a red clip of armor-piercing rounds. All Alice had left was an old handgun in a rear holster, her NYPD day-stick, and a knife. She went for her gun, but they had the drop on her, laser targeting arrays beeping acquisition before she'd got the pistol clear of her back.

This was it.

[10]

"I thought the doorman and elevator attendant were my friends. They had worked here for over twenty years; I gave them ten dollars every Christmas. Now they don't smile when they see me, just scowl and ask for money. It's time I moved into a tower."
Cortex Employee No. 345, interviewed in her Upper West Side apartment, NY, USA 2052

―――

"Since the MI takeover there hasn't been a single aircraft or ship accident. Not one. Great for the insurance companies, less so the legal teams."
Unemployed maritime lawyer, London, 2054

―――

Red never imagined emotions could be so powerful. Terror was a wild animal that shook his body. He couldn't see where he was, the clouds thick as milk, but the cable rose at an angle hard to walk up, let alone crawl along on its ice-glazed surface. He clung to it as if it were a bucking horse, arms and legs wrapped around as far as they would go. His cheek crushed against the icy steel; his body shivered in the squall.

The wind grew in intensity until it became a freezing gale that tore at his frozen fingers. Another roar of air pushed him to the right; if he slid upside down it was game over. His hands were so cold he didn't know if they were frostbitten or just cut to pieces. He clung on with everything he had. The wind calmed. He struggled onward. The pattern repeated.

How long had he been inching upward? Ten minutes? An hour? There was no way he'd deliver on time, and that meant no money.

Focus on the present. No point being rich and dead.

He didn't know where his pursuers were, only that they were gaining on him. They'd shouted at him for a while, but now the wind's roar drowned out everything, turning his world into a bubble of frigid mist that froze his clothes to his skin. His body shook in a last-ditch attempt to stave off exposure; the jerking motion threatened to break his grip.

A tear grew in the surrounding clouds, the storm shifting, and Red saw how high above the bridge he'd climbed. The nanocamoflage nets had been reeled in like sails to save them from the weather. Below him, arrayed under the withdrawn netting, ran a series of long, linear greenhouses glowing with a soft white light. Red's heart ached at the sight of so much space and soil. To their right, a row of metal columns supported a cantilevered landing pad that hung over the river. A large helicopter sat there, rotors turning.

The aircraft looked heavy, as if forged from a single ingot of steel, and capable of taking a lot of gunfire. People scuttled back and forth, carrying coffin-sized boxes to it. They wore weird silver suits, like reactor workers, and the boxes steamed. No, he was wrong: the packages were freezing, their cold turning the damp air into snow.

Clouds smothered him again, but Red had a better idea where he was now. Fear still gripped him but it was no longer paralyzing, and he crept upward, legs, hands, repeating the same movements hundreds of times.

Later.

The storm had blown through, leaving a sunset that painted deep orange over the few remaining clouds. Red had never seen the island like this. As a ground dweller, it was hard for him to comprehend the vista. Manhattan appeared a redwood forest, thousands of narrow trees rising impossibly high, their tips shimmering in the dying sun. Armor-glass domes hundreds of feet across encrusted the towers like drops of water on blades of grass. Verdant parks were just visible inside these blisters, rolling hills silhouetted against the orange clouds.

The view was peaceful, calm.

Red looked back to see his pursuers still following.

He summoned one last burst of energy to approach the top of the tower and saw that the red box was a shipping container boosted from an old boat. It was bolted to the tower's side, big drops of blue molecular resin squeezed out from other connections. Surveillance gear covered the roof; Red recognized parts from police Hoppers, but other than that he had no clue. There were satellite upload dishes, sphere clusters, tall ceramic aerials, and aerostat recharge points. The pure green light of a targeting laser ran over his face; zeroed in on his eye for a retinal scan. They knew all about him now.

The girl at the stall, far below, said this wasn't gang turf. She was wrong. This was a Fourth Ward surveillance station tracking movement across their domain. It looked like they'd hacked into the Scorchers' radio communications and tracked every cop from here. The Ward were rule-obsessed assholes, but they excelled at this high-tech stuff.

Shouts carried on the air so Red resumed his crawl. The white barrier blocked his path; it was a painted lamp post rolled to its side and lashed in place with climber's rope. He crawled to the pole and flopped over it, lungs heaving, body shivering with exertion.

"Hope you saved something for the way back," a deep female voice said.

Red hung there like an animal trophy. He couldn't reply, couldn't lift his head, just raised his hand in a weak wave. There was nothing more, so he concentrated on clearing his mind and stopping the adrenaline flow that shook his body. Minutes crept by before he could push himself upright.

"So it lives. Amazing really, considering that dumb-ass climb." The woman was middle-aged, and wore dirty jeans and a baggy gray sweater. Her large glasses glittered as she smiled and gave him a small nod. "I've seen some stupidity up here, but that was top five. Trouble, huh?"

"They close?" was all Red could pant. He gestured at the cable behind him.

"Yup." She clipped herself to a carabiner welded to the barrier, then edged toward him on a narrow mesh walkway and pulled him upright. "Something to deliver to the island, I guess."

Red knew his mouth had dropped open when she laughed.

"You're not the first kid I've met up here," she said. "Besides, I was a teacher back in the day and can see through adolescent lies in my sleep. I find it best to get to the point."

Red nodded to Manhattan. "I got delivery that end."

"Okay, hold on." She leaned over the drop, a thin, blue cable holding her to the walkway, and cupped her hands around her mouth. "You kids wait there—that's a Fourth Ward instruction."

Angry voices cursed back, but the pursuers stopped their climb.

"Thank you." Red looked at the teacher. "Catch me, they'll kill me."

"I won't let them hurt you, okay? Up here it's my world, but down there ... Well, that's out of my jurisdiction."

As Red opened his mouth to talk, shouts came from far below, followed by gunfire. A deep explosion rattled the walkway. The cable shook with aftershocks and icicles showered him. The teacher shouted, slipped, and fell to spin at the end of her rope as a black, sooty cloud rose to envelop them. The choking smell of burning rubber filled Red's nose. Another detonation hammered the Bridge and he stumbled, flapped for the lamppost, and held on, arms wrapped around the cold steel, feet swinging above the drop.

More gunfire, higher pitched, with a jagged edge that sounded like a chainsaw cutting metal. An alarm, loud, echoing. Tremors shook the cable beneath Red's arms, mild at first but then so violent that his vision blurred, the world becoming a series of still images.

The teacher reached for him.

She was shouting, but he couldn't hear.

His hands slipped.

He fell.

[11]

"Building off-world civilizations is an essential part of species survival."
President Rachael Harper, State of the Union address, Washington DC, 2054

"We need a new approach to childcare and protection. The ongoing mass unemployment, and subsequent loss of child life, could pose a significant challenge to our reelection efforts."
Department of Homeland Security and Employment report, "Eyes Only,"
President of the United States, 2054

"China's augmented-human trial drastically outperforms our own military programs. It is logical to assume they will employ these new

assets system-wide. If we don't act now, we could lose any grip we have on the future."
Pentagon Report, "War in the Age of Sentient Machines," President of the United States, 2053

THE ROOM CONROY ENTERED WAS A PERFECT REPRESENTATION of minimal architecture: red-oak floor, raw plaster walls, and illuminated white ceiling. Every surface separated from its neighbor by a half-inch shadow gap, the dark lines creating floating planes of material. A table filled the center space, a triangle of low-iron glass held aloft on four cast-alloy legs. Three Mies chairs, chrome and black leather, faced each other. Two were occupied, the avatars matching their owner's true appearance.

New York's mayor was a handsome middle-aged man with a close-cropped beard, white teeth, and crisp gray Armani suit. The Pentagon's head of biomechanical research looked very different. She was short and wide, with her straw-blond hair in the eternal Marines buzz cut. Her face was untouched by war, but both her arms carried vivid blue reprint tags from a field hospital printer. They projected from her military uniform like broken sticks, the crude pixilation of her skin a badge of honor.

Conroy took the third seat. "Mayor Thornley, General Alisson, I apologize for the delay."

"No trouble, I assume?" General Alisson said. There was a hint of data-compression in her voice, the treble clipped.

"Trouble, but not troubling. We undertook Officer Squire's extraction this morning. I will be questioning him later."

"Good. If the UN knows before we are ready, this is over," Alisson said.

"I understand," Conroy said. *Is that all it takes to ascend in the military? To be a mouthpiece for the apparent and dull?*

"Is the delivery on schedule?" she said.

"Yes, everything is proceeding per our agreement. The first one hundred are en route to West Point for review and testing. I have a further five on ice pending their field trial permits." Conroy turned to the mayor. "Once I receive military approval, it will take another month to complete the initial batch. Being forced to use that old helicopter, of course, slows the delivery."

"I understand your dislike, but I can't have anything logged into air traffic control. The chopper is off record, and we will continue with it for now." The mayor's voice held a faint Brooklyn drawl.

"How is everything else?" Conroy said.

"The printing of redesigned and augmented humans still remains a federal offense, if that's what you're asking."

"And?" Conroy clenched his fists. Thornley spoke so slowly, it always took ten questions when one should do. It was hard not to reach over and strangle his avatar.

"Politics is invariably a compromise—you understand that, Mr. Bank," Thornley said. "I've not announced trials yet, as certain associated parties want the riots to start before any press releases."

Associated parties—the other New York families, you mean. As if I don't know all about your little side deals. Conroy settled back in his chair. There was no point forcing this conversation; all he would do is make them defensive. He needed them for now, so it was best to act that way. "Of course, and I await your schedule," he said.

The mayor smiled back. "Patience, Patsy. Once the Augments are on the streets, the increased health and welfare spending will quash any dissent."

"You're sure you can control the debates?" Alisson asked. Thornley ignored her.

"How is the military schedule?" Conroy said.

Alisson consulted her uniform; white text scrolled across her sleeve. "A month for the full trials. If the reprints work to specification, I see no reason why we can't move straight to production. Fourth Ward can instigate the riots in thirty days, plus or minus."

"What about the president?" Conroy asked Thornley. *If you can't see she's the wild card here, you're an idiot.*

"The mayor's office can unilaterally call a state emergency. It's protocol for us to consult the White House, but not law. She'll get involved—too many financial donors here—but I have the authority to request unilateral military intervention. The city's budget is a bigger challenge; six weeks and New York is bankrupt."

"That should be enough," Alisson said. "*If* Fourth Ward can keep the heat on the streets."

"Food is already constrained. When I close the Bridge's markets, things will tip. Don't worry, there's no way the NYPD will cope once this gets going," Conroy said.

"I need the switchover complete in six months. The NYPD has to be off the city books by then."

"I can deliver my side of the agreement," Conroy said to the mayor. "You abide by yours?"

"Yes, yes, of course. How many times do I need to answer this? Deliver, and your precious family will get its legal status approved. Now, if there is no other business, I have a press conference to attend."

"One more thing," Conroy said.

"What?"

"The Bridge's lease is up end of the year. I need to know where we are on this."

"Do your job and the mayor's office will approve a motion to extend all bridge and tunnel business parks for another five years. Good enough?"

Conroy said nothing; he stared at the mayor, who fidgeted, nodded, and closed his Virt session.

"What do you think of him?" Conroy said to Alisson.

"New York has over twenty-seven million people on or below the starvation line. He has to try something new."

"Are your investments secure?"

"As long as you deliver, and the reprints do their job, I shall spin the department off as a research incubator by year's end."

"What will you do with all the money?"

"You don't expect me to live on the ground forever, do you?"

"No ma'am," Conroy said and removed his visors.

His quarters were small and cramped, the air stuffy. He sipped a glass of cold water; took two painkillers. The edges of a headache pulsed behind his eyes. This had already been a long day, and there was still so much to do.

[12]

"World gettin' colder, people gettin' colder. You gotta adapt, see?"
Five Points hitman "Candy Pops," Manhattan, 2053

———

"Look around yourself, then tell me the MI revolution is a bad thing."
Cortex Employee No. 37, speaking from her Caribbean island, 2053

———

Red had never fallen to his death before, so didn't know what to do. In the end he settled on a mixture of flailing about and screaming. Something grabbed his arm and flipped him over until he had no idea what was up or down. The multicolored coral of the Bridge's construction spun around him.

Another grab, then another. Each time his velocity dropped as a thin and hard line dragged against him.

The next one stuck across his chest; it was a strand from the bird-catcher nets. Their composite fibers were capable of extreme deformation: really stretchy *and* sticky.

Red crashed through another net, and it fastened to him like a spider's web, slowing his fall. Then another, another. He spun and saw people below him, three in a line, facing off against someone dressed in black. He couldn't move, couldn't shout, the cocoon smothering him as he struck the three people like a bowling ball, knocking the center person out cold.

He came to a rest facing a woman dressed in black. She moved with a machined elegance to draw a huge silver gun from a rear holster. She fired from her hip like an old-school cowboy, the noise deafening. Her wrist flexed, absorbing the recoil; she fired again, again, her aim unerring. The jeeks either side did a weird dance as they took the bullets, and fell away to leave Red trussed and gagged in front of the woman.

"Not what I had planned," she said and ran to him. "Thanks, kid. You okay?"

"Hmmmm. Mm. *Mmmm*," was all he could manage.

"Why are you asking him questions? Why? Am I the only one who can see he's unable to communicate?"

Red couldn't tell where the second voice came from, but it was quiet and distorted like a blown speaker.

"Not being able to talk is an appealing personality trait right now, why don't you try it?" the woman said into her jacket collar. The only people who wore SWAT gear this smart were Scorchers or Cosa Nostra, and she looked Japanese or something, *definitely* not Sicilian. What the hell was a cop doing here? She had to be part of a larger team, which would explain the explosions.

"Not your best reply," her clothing said, then went quiet.

The woman kneeled and flexed her wrist in an odd movement; a long white dagger dropped into her hand. She was a Scorcher then: the ceramic blade had the blue NYPD logo stamped on its side. She slipped it under part of the catcher nets and cut upward in a fast, sure stroke. The pressure on Red's chest lessened, and she flipped him over like a dead fish and did the same to his back. There was tugging, a *snap*, and his arms came free.

He heard shouting in the distance as ricochets fizzed around them.

"Kid, I leave you here, they'll finish the job. Hold on."

She rolled him back over, grabbed the webbing across his chest, and dragged him like a burst suitcase into the alleyway. Gloom descended as soon as they rounded the corner, sky visible in flashes through the bundles of cables that spanned the space.

The woman was thin and strong, built like an athlete, but Red could tell she was hurt. Her body sagged to the right, and she kept rubbing her lower ribcage, gasping in pain. He used his free hand to tear at the webbing covering his face.

"Cut me out. I can move fast," he said.

The cop looked back up the alley, gnawing her lip, then stopped and bent to the task. "Stay still. You twitch, I could end up cutting you."

"You're a Scorcher, right?"

"That a problem? You don't look like Fourth Ward either."

"No, I'm freelance, got a job, just passing though. Where's your team? Think I can hitch a ride out?" Red knew to never trust a cop, but it was worth asking if it saved your life.

"I'm on my own in here."

"What? This is the Fourth Ward. You can't be here by yourself."

"They've got my partner, but I can't get backup without evidence proving he was kidnapped."

"I thought Scorchers looked after each other."

"You're supposed to, but then you're not. It's a judgement call—hell, I don't know. Ask my boss if I still have one."

She cut the last of the strands and Red struggled upright. He was bruised but okay, though his jacket was a mess. Most of the album artwork he'd spent hours on was gone, which was a real pisser.

"You should disappear, kid," she said. "Sticking with me will raise your health insurance premiums." She ejected the gun's clip and loaded new rounds with red markings. "Things are going to get ballistic before they get better."

What to do? He looked around. He'd seen the Bridge from up high, and there was no way through down here. If he was going to deliver, he needed help.

"You're a cop, yeah? So you have to protect me, right? I need to get to the island."

She looked at him long and hard, sighed, clicked her collar. "Suit, call in a rescue team to pick him up. Any contractor will do, charge my card."

"Don't forget your rent is due and you require two new ribs. We don't want a mess like last time, do we?" her jacket said.

"It's an extraction—pick him up, drop him off the other side. Can't be that much."

There was a moment's silence; Red wiped his sticky hands on the wall.

"That's annoying," the jacket said. "Communications are being jammed. It's sophisticated as well—smells like military gear to me."

"Local or wide?"

"From the scale of the Bridge, I'd guess wide. See if your aerostat can get high enough to send a message."

"For once a good idea." The cop pulled a small black drone from her pocket, shook it, put it away. "Except it took a round somewhere."

"Well then, you'll have to climb and see if we can get a clear signal higher up. Obvious if you think about it for more than a second."

Red knew the clothing wasn't alive in an MI way, but it sounded so human that he smiled.

"Mike's tracker came from the upper decks; drop the kid off and go in for him?" she said.

"If we must."

The cop turned to Red. "What's your name?"

"Red."

"I'm Officer Yu, though I suggest you call me Alice while we're in here. I can't get you out right now, but you're welcome to join me or go your own way."

"I'll come," Red said. He would drop her the moment it got bad, but she *had* offered to get him out.

"Let's go." She turned and headed away into the dank alley.

RED FOLLOWED Alice as she worked her way through a network of alleys. He was lost in moments. At first every unit and street looked the same, but he started to notice differences. Some units were clean and new, lights bright in the twilight. Others, deeper in, were dark and dirty, uneven floor filled with brackish puddles that stank of oil and coolants. There were rich and poor here, just like everywhere else.

"Where we headed?" he asked, panting. Alice set a hard pace.

"We need to get back inside, there are too many eyes out here." She stopped at a junction box. "But I don't know enough about the interior layout to tell if there is a prison cell or fusion reactor behind this wall. I'm looking for a maintenance doorway, something that will put us back into the low-level ductwork."

Ahead of them lay a collection of rusted yellow shipping containers, and behind that rose the tall gray facade of the Bridge's cooling system. It was warmer here, soft rain dripping from the network of overhead cables. Somewhere close by, hot metal ticked as it cooled, and the floor vibrated with distant machinery. They'd not seen anyone in minutes. The sun faded to leave them in blue darkness. Crimson lights glowed to life, the oil-rig-sized superstructure edged with ship's lighting.

"We move up there and bust our way through the first entrance we come to." She pointed to a metal service wall near to the vertical ducts, and set off.

At the next junction, food stores and a bar formed a small town square. Janky electronic music drifted from the beer shack, which had a busted neon sign out front flickering *Unknown Pleasures* in a font Red didn't recognize. Two old women sat on its porch, drinking oily yellow liquid from jam jars. Alice beckoned for Red to stop, but he stepped past her, and approached the ladies.

"I like the name of your bar," he said.

"We don't serve kids. Get lost," one of the crones said.

"We're looking for a way though, no questions. She can pay." Red pointed at Alice, except there was a hole in the universe where the cop had been moments ago.

The women looked at each other, cackled, and approached him.

"What's a little chicken like you doin' out here all alone? Where's your mama?"

The mention of his absent mother made Red blush, anger and shame mixing.

"Aww, lookit him," the other woman said and took a deep swig of the clear drink; she stank of paint thinners and old apples. "He's blushing. Poor little boy. You looking for a good time? That the deal?"

Red looked around for Alice, but she was long gone. Icicles formed in his blood as he edged backward. "No, nothing like that. I need a way through to the island is all."

"Little chick want a guide? What you think, June?" One crone nodded to the other.

"I think his pecker ain't up to use yet, is what I think. He better turn over his pocket money right now, as I'm getting thirsty."

Red tried to run, but the women were quick and grabbed at him. They were horribly strong, their thin arms fueled by liquor. The one called June pinned him against a faded steel wall, cold and hard against his back. The other started to search his pockets. He kicked out, struggled. "Get off me, I'm warning you." But his words rang hollow.

"Well lookit this." The second woman held up the letter, its clean, yellow rectangle at odds with the surroundings.

Seeing it in her hands made Red crazy, and he writhed, out of control. "Give it back, that's mine."

June banged him against the wall; his vision sparkled and blood filled his mouth.

"Kick me one more time, boy, and I'll cut you slow, let you bleed out on the floor, you dig?"

Red said nothing.

"Okay, let's see what else you gots." Next she found his five dollars. Both women cackling with joy at their unexpected windfall. That was it, all he had. June let him go and he slumped onto the hard floor.

"Please, give it back."

"Nah, finders keepers. You still want a way through?" June said.

"Not without that."

"There you go then, we done you a favor, yeah? There's no passage to the island here, it's a dead end to any non–Fourth Warders. You're better off running home, boy. Go, git."

"At last, something useful from this conversation." Alice stepped behind the two women and placed a long, telescopic black rod against June's neck. There was a blue flash, and the old hag did the electric jitterbug and fell to the deck with a bang. The stink of cooked meat and cordite filled the air.

"Now then," Alice said to the other woman without a pause, "I believe you have this young boy's five dollars. He offered money in exchange for information, you have replied in kind. Take it, and return to your nasty little life. Pretend you never saw us. Say anything, I'll come back here and burn your shitty bar down into slag. Do we have a deal?"

Alice's sudden appearance had left the other woman stunned. She looked between Alice and Red, eyes bulging, then down at the money in her fist. That broke her spell, the pale blue note meant a big night for her. She nodded at Alice, gave Red a lifeless stare, and slinked into the shadows.

Alice tossed her day stick, its battery dead, and plucked the letter from the unconscious woman's grip. She read the address, face cracking in surprise, and turned to Red. "Who the hell knows Charles Takamatsu?"

"This barkeep in Brooklyn. Dive called the Crazy Horse."

"Interesting."

Red pushed away from the wall, flicked his collar up, and took the letter. "Why the hell you let her take my money? That was mine."

"We all need money, kid. Figured a lesson was more important."

"Oh please, do educate me," he tried to sneer, but just sounded young and out of his depth.

"There are more ways to buy something than money. Look around, what do you see?"

Red didn't bother to turn his head. "It's a wrecked bridge full of turds crawling over each other."

"Wrong. This is a *family*. They're in it together. The ones that live here won't sell Bank out for cash—not the amount we have, anyway."

"Then we're screwed."

"No we're not. Come on."

Alice turned and ran with a skipping gait that Red tried to match. There was a sourness in his mouth, guilt over his mother's demands ever present: clothes, food, drink, on and on, an eternal shopping list. He'd failed to keep the money but he would make the mail drop no matter the consequences.

Alice led him to the tall metal wall that rattled with a low hum. A locked door punctured its side. She used her smart key to open it and they slipped though into the cold, dark silence.

[13]

"It was fine up here, just fine, until the printers came online. After that we became just another resource to fight over."
Dina Brekeridge, number seventeen of the "Hundred First" Martian settlers, Erebus Montes, Mars, 2051

———

"We underestimated them. Who knew a bunch of scientists would be so clever?"
General Sisko, Colonial Marines press briefing, Mars, 2052

———

THE STIMULANT COMEDOWN WAS AS BRUTAL AS ALICE FEARED, muscles shaking with fatigue, throat slick with a sour aftertaste. She ignored the pain and pushed on through the tunnels, looking for a way up. It was cold and dark, the round steel walls dimly lit by red emergency packs epoxied to the ceiling. She was running on automatic, with plans that amounted to nothing more than to get higher, try to find Mike, call in a Hopper. Outside, things had seemed simpler; inside her claustrophobia returned, fueled by deadening exhaustion. The weight of the Bridge was a tactile presence, oil and metal in her mouth. The urge to succumb to blind panic, run, *get out,* pushed against her like an invisible hand. Only her bloody-minded stubbornness kept her upright and moving.

That and the kid. Now she had responsibilities that went beyond the professional requirements of her job. Red had no chance down here alone. They'd be dragging his body from the Hudson's fish nets within days, use his corpse for fuel in the city furnaces.

"Suit, still have Mike's location?"

She squeezed through another tight corner, the space crisscrossed by hundreds of power and data cables wrapped together in clear tape.

"Of course. I would say if we lost touch," Suit sniffed back.

"But no map, huh?"

"I'm a Series-Three smart-system. Conjuring information from the ether is beyond my skill set."

"So no map, then."

"None. Besides, look at this place. I bet no one has any idea how to get from one end to the other anymore. Any initial organizing principal has been long since lost."

The tunnel funneled sound toward them. The high-pitched hiss of Alice's tinnitus was complemented by rumbling machinery that clunked and chewed, along with what could have been gunfire. Tension crept up from her stomach, bunching her shoulders.

She shook her head.

This was familiar. She'd been in here before.

But had she?

She knew where she was.

But did she?

Beyond a certain threshold, pain did weird things to the brain, spawning alternate realities for the consciousness to hide inside, a pocket of calm in a world of agony. Alice had fallen into one on Mars, the fugue state a refuge from her injuries. She'd climbed out over time, drugs and therapy the ladder.

But what if she was still there, in that fugue, in that fire, burning? Nothing like the Bridge existed when she'd first lived in New York. Was this feverish, fairy-tale architecture the imagining of a dying mind?

She stopped. Red ran into her back with an *oof*.

Remember your therapy, remember the notes in your pocket. There were no post-its on Mars. Remember your apartment here, how you've plastered it with those yellow squares, each one telling you this is real. Sure, that means you can't bring anyone home, let them see how you live, but that's a small price to pay to anchor your life.

(What if someone made you face your illness? You can't, can you?)

Focus on the notes, feel them in your jacket. You are here, this is real. Take one out—never mind the kid. Stick it on the tunnel walls. Could you do that if you're dead, dying?

"What is it?" Red said, his voice quiet. Water dripped in the background. "See someone?"

Alice ignored him, took the yellow pad from her pocket. Her hands shook. There, on the cover in her fine script, *This Is Reality*. She peeled it off, stuck it onto the curved wall where it fluttered in the ever-present breeze. She looked back over her shoulder, Red's ridiculous rooster tail of a haircut in her way.

This wasn't Mars. That had been worse, much, much worse.

MARTIAN INDEPENDENT REPUBLIC, 2052

ALICE LANDED, bounced, came to rest upside down, face pressing against something cold and smooth. Her neck was twisted sideways, shoulder muscles trembling under the load, pain building along her spine. Hot blood thudded in her head, each beat accompanied by a jagged spike of agony. At first all she could hear was a roaring hiss, then the crackling of fire and the popping of burning munitions grew loud.

The dark stench of scorched metal and burning meat filled her mouth, her nostrils.

Alice tried to open her eyes but couldn't, the impact foam still covering her face. The ejection seat had squirted the oxygenated foam down her throat to prevent internal injury. As she struggled, it melted to leave a sickly residue tasting of laboratories and solvents.

Alice spat and saliva dripped up her cheeks. She tried to twist her head but found herself wedged against something too heavy to move. The ejection seat's frame and straps gripped like a straitjacket, making it hard to breathe. The final layer melted from her eyes and she opened them, wincing in the pale light. Her face was pressed against the boulevard's smooth, gray concrete. It shook under her, a deep explosion somewhere below. There was a high-pitched hiss of escaping gas, and the unmistakable *whoosh* of incoming orbital missile fire. She tried to move, couldn't.

The impact was deafening, the shockwave lifting and tossing her away like a leaf. She tumbled, up, down, light, dark, came to rest on her side.

That was better—her now-free hands searched for the harness clip. It stuck at first, the ceramic bent, then undid with a click. She scrambled out of the seat. Her balance was off, Martian gravity less than half that of Earth's. Blood trickled under her helmet and down her face. The boulevard was wide, its outer edge boarded by the lake, the inner a ten-foot-tall wall capped by the Parliament building's metal roof.

Alice rose to a crouch, groaning in pain, and ran to the wall. She unslung and assembled her gun as she looked around. Where was everyone? There was nothing apart from the empty street and burning forest. The flames were louder, heat on her skin, smoke in her eyes and mouth. The dome had resealed itself, the central hexagon traced with yellow lines as its smart tech rebonded. The panel beside it had two small holes in its center: needle missiles fired from the *Fucker*. They wouldn't have done that unless things had really gone to shit. For the first time Alice considered the possibility that all three drop-ships had come down. Smoke collected above her, thick and black, curling and twisting with the rising heat.

She checked her comms gear. Her visor was long gone, and her helmet gave nothing but garbled chatter, its smart-systems wrecked by whatever weapon had taken out the *It's Been A Long Week*. She looked back; the wall curved from sight. There was no sign of her ship, but the crackle of burning munitions came from ahead. She chewed her lip, made a decision and moved forward in a low crouch, every few seconds stopping and checking around her.

Nothing.

She wanted to call out, shout, but bit down on her tongue. She'd been alone most of her life, but, for the first time, the Marines made her part of a team. She would locate her ship, find any survivors, and work out a way to fulfill her mission.

She inched forward, gun ready, trying to get used to the lower gravity. The crackle of small explosions and the smell of burning metal grew. Further around the dome, she saw marks on the concrete boulevard. Light at first, a thin white scratch that grew as she moved forward. The scratch became a gouge, a tear, the color shifting from white, to gray, then black. It was the impact line of something moving fast. She abandoned her crouch and jogged forward, scanning for IEDs.

Nothing.

Then she saw it. The *Long Week* had come out of its fall, but too late. At the end of the impact line was a crater in the hard surface. She couldn't see inside, but thick black smoke poured upward, and the yellow flash and crackle of burning ordnance popped from inside. Splintered composite panels surrounded the hole like scattered confetti. She saw one, then two bodies crumpled into bundles of shattered bones. She ran to the first. It was Miller, his neck broken, blank eyes open to the stars. She placed his head back with care and ran to the next body. This was better: Reynolds was breathing but unconscious. Alice stripped the ejection seat from the woman, ignored her broken legs, and raised her in a fireman's lift. Reynolds weighed under half her Earth amount, but her mass remained the same. Alice stumbled, adjusting, then ran back to the wall and laid the Marine against the stone. The leg breaks weren't the only damage. Reynolds stomach was swollen and hard, her skin pale. Alice took out an anesthetic stick and stabbed it into the woman's neck. It discharged with a low hiss. Alice was about to head back to the crater when Reynolds grabbed her.

"Yu?"

"Hey, Reynolds. You're alive, just need to hang in there, okay? I've got to check the rest of the ship."

"What hit us?"

"No idea. Something new, a better EMP, not sure. Take this."

Alice handed Reynolds her reserve pistol, then set off for the downed craft. The inferno intensified as she approached. The ship had caught fully now, its thick plastic walls burning with a choking smoke that made Alice drop and crawl to the crater's edge. The aircraft was pulverized beyond recognition. Structural spars stuck upward like broken tree trunks, bright silver components visible through orange flames. Every so often, a red camouflage panel curled up and sublimed as she watched. There was no way anyone was still alive in there, but Alice had to be sure. She rose, ready to inch into the fire, when there was another explosion. Hot shrapnel sizzled against her body armor, and the shockwave flipped her over to face the dark sky.

A flare twinkled above her, distant and cold.

"Incoming—" she screamed and rolled into a ball, hands over her helmet as the needle missiles slashed into the lake. The ground lifted and flicked her upward in a devastating *ka-thump*. She smacked down on her side, saw billowing clouds of steam shoot skyward from the water. The ground shook again, and a deep hiss penetrated the roaring in her ears. The lake rippled, shuddered, then drained away into an open crack in the dome's foundations. More steam billowed upward, huge clouds that swirled and mixed with the roiling smoke. It started to rain in hot, black drops that splattered over the concrete and drenched her. The foul liquid stung her eyes, found every crack in her armor. Bitter oil filled her mouth, the smell of charred pork seared her nostrils.

Alice rolled to her front and then rose into a crouch. The hiss of escaping steam and crackle of the burning ship was deafening. She couldn't see the containment vessel from where she squatted, so scuttled around the lip of the crater, keeping as close to the ground as she could. The wreckage was clearer from the other side. The vessel had split like an egg, its walls showing only three ejection holes. The rest were sealed. The Marines on board had been unable to get out.

Alice kneeled, put her hand on the hot concrete and threw up.

She tried her comms gear again, but got nothing but garbled feedback. She pulled a targeting beacon from her belt, clicked the activation button, peeled the glue strip and stuck it to the crater's side. The *Fucker* wouldn't send its last drop ship down here, not with some new weapon on the loose, but she didn't know what else to do.

She ran back to Reynolds.

The woman was dead.

NEW YORK, 2055

"ALICE, WHAT IS IT?" There was an edge of hysteria in Red's voice.

She shook herself, focused on his pale white face, the thin features pulled into a frown, and forced the terrible memories aside. Her body shivered, slick with sweat, fear a bitter tang in her mouth. She closed her eyes, imagined the claustrophobia as heat in her lungs, and blew it out and away. Doing this in her veteran therapy sessions had been embarrassing, now it gave some small relief.

"I'm not at my best in small spaces."

A hand grabbed hers in the dim light, held on tight, anchoring her.

"Thanks, kid. Okay, time to go."

They continued to the end of the duct. A six-foot-tall mesh grille was bolted over an array of fist-sized fans that shrieked as they pushed noxious air outward. The smell of hot plastic and stale antiseptic was strong; Alice recognized it from somewhere. Hospital? Mars? She didn't want to know, forced it away, her brush with the past all too fresh in her mind.

A metal ladder led to a maintenance door in the ceiling. She scaled and lifted the hatch an inch. The corridor that greeted her looked like the inside of a submarine designed for three-foot-tall people; packed full of pipes and cables, it shimmered with heat. Alice nodded down at Red, put a finger to her lips, and beckoned for him to follow. As he started up, she slipped through and squatted in the stale heat.

"Suit?"

"Still have a track but there's a lot of weird interference."

She checked her wrist display. What next? Red's question about what she was doing here had struck a nerve. He'd been right—weren't cops supposed to look after their own? What was the point of being one otherwise? Since their jacking, her whole mission had been compromised by the leaden weight of keeping her job. When had she changed so much? As a runner, a Marine, the lives of her team members meant as much as her own. She'd risked herself over and again to save her family; now she was looking for a pay cheque to heal her ribs, cover the rent, rather than to save her partner. What if Mike had obeyed orders and left her the countless times she'd screwed up?

No.

She forced herself to stop the spiral. Lose focus in here, she'd become just another name etched into the NYPD's wall of honorable fallen.

She could still make it out of here and keep her job, save Mike, but she needed a plan.

It was time to talk to Red.

[14]

"Manhattan's bridges are no-go zones for citizen and police alike. Only capitalism can fix that. You hear me, Silicon Valley? Big pharma? Bioweapon start-ups? You can do anything you want, to anyone you want, as long as you stay within set confines and pay your taxes."
New York City Mayor Jonathon Thornley, speech to Wall Street CEOs, NY, USA, 2053

"Smart clothing will allow us to reduce boots on the ground lowering engagement costs. Also, as the clothing is more durable than the human component, it can be reused when the original wearer is end-of-life."
Pentagon Report, "War in the Age of Sentient Machines," President of the United States, 2053

Conroy took a sip of chilled water, ice clinking in the glass. His headache remained, a low throb at the base of his skull that spiked when he nodded at the screen. "Their progress is remarkable when you consider everything. Look at the boy. What is it about the letter that makes him so desperate to deliver? He's nothing but a bad attitude in a big jacket. Tell me, Michael, what would you do with him?"

"Short or long term?" Squire said.

"Long term, of course. The largest challenge I face as an employer of young people is their ignorance of timescales. So many fail to appreciate significant change requires years of effort. I ask again, what would you do if you had him for, say, the next five years?"

Conroy watched Squire with a strong sense of love and frustration. They were opposites in so many ways; Conroy short and squat like a weight lifter, Squire tall and elegant like a nineteen-fifties movie star. Squire sat across the table dressed in mismatched clothing, sunflowers bobbing like slow-motion sparks behind him. One-Eye stood at Conroy's shoulder. They needed no further protection; military-grade drones hovered with quiet determination. A screen showed grainy security-cam footage of Alice and Red talking. There was no audio, Alice's escape having taken out One-Eye's aerostat.

"You've met my children many times, Patsy," Squire said. Conroy nodded. "You know what being a father teaches you?"

"Evidently not."

"Your life means nothing in the end."

"Are you saying this boy's life is worth more than your own?"

"No, I'm saying the older I get, the less important my wishes become."

"I don't believe you think that, but we digress and time grows short. Answer my question."

Squire turned back to the screen, frowned, chewed the tip of his index finger. "The boy has a style of his own, doesn't look to be a follower. That shows individuality combined with the stubbornness to stand apart. I can't tell intelligence levels from here, but the detail and care taken to paint his jacket suggests curiosity and patience. That being the case, we have a creative, smart, stubborn boy used to looking after himself. I would try to protect that aspect while reintegrating him with society. Not school—I doubt how relevant that would be. A local gang, perhaps, one where I could keep an eye on him."

"A runner?"

"No." Squire paused. "Maybe supervision, give him a mail route to organize, see how he adapts to deadlines and responsibilities."

"And how would you integrate him into your home?"

"What are you getting at? I understand I've upset you, but—" Squire stopped as Conroy raised a finger to his lips. He changed tack. "Susan is my oldest."

"Ten?"

"Eleven, crazy as that is. I'd let her supervise him."

"Not Peter?"

"No, Peter's too shy. He'd be influenced by the kid's dress sense."

"So the interaction with this boy would change your family, as well as the other way around."

Squire shrugged, not liking where this was headed. "You're twisting my words here."

"Indulge me."

"Okay. A family, in the traditional sense, is a self-contained unit. Self-referencing systems tend toward their own rules and regulations. They can be hard and insular—say religious doctrine—or soft, where they embrace the world and trust their values will sustain."

"How does your own self-contained system, your family, interact with others?"

"Well, you can't live on your own, especially these days, right?" Squire gave a dry laugh that dropped dead on the floor.

"No, especially these days," Conroy said. "When your family interacts with others, how does it work?"

Squire was silent for a moment, his breath loud. "What is it, Patsy? What have I done?"

Conroy watched his face in the quiet that followed, traced emotions as they roiled below the surface. "It's an omission, a lack of having done, that we will discuss in time." Conroy placed the glass back on the table. The room was silent apart from the faint hiss of the drones and the occasional creak of stretching metal. "I understand you are police, but what I'm interested in learning is how you and yours go about an everyday existence."

"I do the introductions," Squire said. He sat, resigned, knew the truth was his only way out. "Most of the neighbors want to be our friends because they think I can help them. Some knew me before the phase change, think that makes a difference. I help in little ways, get extra water rations, or more time to pay for food. Once I've got to know them, checked them out with Central Dispatch, I let Samantha deal with any negotiations. We trade my protection for their goods and services."

"You delegate responsibilities for the interactions after your initial review?"

"That's a technical way of putting it, but yes."

"So, if you had someone to introduce you to more people, you could extend the range of your help. Bring more families under your wing."

"I guess, but that's not what I want, never did. Power does nothing for me, I just want my day to day to stay the same, do a shift and then be with my family."

"Then why don't you franchise?"

Squire frowned. "What do you mean?"

"Find another suitable cop, and add them to your team. They pay you to help build your network."

"That how you've done all this?" Squire looked around.

"In a way, one person at a time." Conroy reached down and removed his composite foot; scratched his stump. It always itched when he was tired. He placed it on the table with a light *clack*, the fabric's weave glinting under the overhead lights. "Power is like roots from a tree, fractal, each piece linking to its neighbor. That is our next step, you see. The Bridge is becoming a franchise, my family splitting and seeding other zones across the country; east, west, and north to start. Vincent here"—he nodded to One-Eye—"will take his leave soon, to the misty waters of the Bay Area. The Golden Gate aggregated long before we did, though that is based around residential units, not a factory such as this one. Do you understand what I'm telling you?"

Squire looked at Conroy, then shook his head. "No."

"America is nothing but a rusting hulk taking in water. You, me, we, need to jump ship, start over. Think the union will hold? Another five years at the most, then all we will have is each other. Fourth Ward is building the future now. Here, San Francisco, Chicago. But like anything under construction we remain vulnerable to weaknesses, internal and out. Any rotting structural member could bring the edifice tumbling down; the liar, the cheat, the diseased spar that corrupts. The once friend who now betrays."

"You talk as if I had a choice," Squire said at last. "That's not what happened."

Conroy turned to the video feed. "What do you think of her?"

"She's nothing special, just your typical veteran trying to stay alive."

"A nobody capable of fighting her way onto the Bridge? That makes no sense. She is a person of *talent*, Michael, someone an old friend should have told me about long before this face to face."

"We've only worked together a few months."

"Twelve."

"I can control her."

"Does this look like *control*?" Conroy's voice rose to a shout; his hands gripped the table edge, knuckles white. With an effort he withdrew into himself, tucked his emotions away. "Do you think I feel safe and secure with her loose?"

Squire stood, face red in the soft light. "If *you* hadn't jacked me, if you'd just called like any normal person, she'd be at home now, saving up for a Virt fuck or whatever she does. *You're* the one that insisted on these theatrics."

"Your disrespect had reached a level where no sit-down would suffice."

Squire's skin was pale as if cast from old wax. "Is that what this is? One last conversation?"

Conroy looked at the screen. The gritty black-and-white display showed the woman and boy moving through a tunnel. They came to a ladder; the woman consulted a wrist screen, then moved upward as smooth as oiled smoke.

"Is our business complete?" he said to One-Eye.

"Yes sir. General Alisson has all but one shipment; those are being printed now. We had a problem with plasma on the last batch, some form of pollutant, and had to refinish them. Per the agreement, we withheld five for our own trials, three patchworks and two augments. They are in Niner's cold room awaiting activation."

"How many do you suggest?"

One-Eye looked at the screen and hesitated. "She seems original, no reprinted parts. Speed and stamina, but limited strength and little imagination. I'd suggest one patchwork."

"Make it one of each."

"Capture or kill?" One-Eye said.

Conroy turned to Squire. "Well, that is up to you, isn't it?"

[15]

"The first major change to city planning was, of course, fully autonomous vehicles. Once people divested themselves of car ownership, parking structures and street edges became new urban playgrounds.
The second major change was the Dyson engine. Overnight personal aerial transportation was a fact of life, and only vestigial car use remained at surface level.
What had appeared a boon to town planning—the reemergence of a bucolic existence among the streets—was unfortunately soon destroyed by the wave of unemployment. What could have been canals and urban parks became shanty towns for the homeless.
With street crime rising, and the viability of aerial transport, it was no surprise when the wealthy moved into high-rise towers. The challenge facing those left behind is how to re-humanize ground level within our severely limited budgets."
Simon Bellerin, "Urban Design in the Age of Automation", RIBA Lecture, London, 2050

Alice held up a hand; Red sagged to the floor, legs splayed in front of him, large boots catching the bright lights. Her ribs throbbed, her legs trembled, and her jaw was swollen from the onset of major stim withdrawal. She forced herself upright and checked for supplies. There was only the knife, pistol and Bunny Bopper left. The gun was loaded with plastic shrapnel rounds, and she had a clip of ricochets in her right thigh pocket. After that, she'd be holding off Fourth Ward with a bad attitude and body odor.

"What are you doing?" Red said.

She looked at him in more detail. The punk hair made him seem older, but he was young and thin, acne only just starting. His milky-white skin was increasingly rare in New York, and his clothing was strange. It wasn't from the streets, but didn't look gang affiliated either.

"Why do you dress like that?" she said.

Red looked down at himself, puzzled. "What do you mean?"

"You don't look street smart, more like a historical photo."

"Good. It took time to get this right." He nodded over his shoulder. "That painting is radio waves from an old record cover. This is my uncle's jacket; he did the back, I did the front. Taught guitar back in the day, now he kinda just sits around keeping out of trouble."

"What does 'bollocks' mean?" She nodded to the white-painted lettering on his arms. He said nothing, just looked at her like she was a total idiot. "Okay, let's start over. What was your plan when you came in here?"

"Why d'you want to know?"

Alice sighed. Even after a year, people's distrust of her uniform hurt. She was a cop, sure, but that didn't mean she had an ulterior motive to everything she did.

"Because I'm lost," she said, "I'm scared, and I don't know what to do next, okay?" She watched him struggle to believe her. "I was a runner too, Red, back in the day."

"Bollocks."

"I'm telling you the truth Red—as a kid I was smart enough to realize I was nothing special. My dad was an asshole from day one."

Red nodded. "I know the feeling."

"He got what he deserved, the bastard. Mom was sweet until cancer paid a visit. After that Paulie and me—that's my brother—found ourselves in one of the orphanages."

"Heard those places were black holes. You did good to get out."

"Be careful what you wish for. Being thirteen, legal guardian to your younger brother, and living on the streets was no Disneyland. I got a job running for the Mac's down in Bay Ridge. Took me a few years, but I grifted my way up to infiltration, got jobs cleaning houses for the Ones. Once inside, I'd steal their encryption keys, clean them out. The bosses took everything I earned and bought themselves places in the towers, left us behind."

"Figures. You can't trust anyone, especially crooks. I don't want anything to do with them or being a runner. First job I applied for was working an old rag-n-bone franchise out in Bay Ridge. Two hundred kids were lined up by the time I got there. I asked this jeek how early I should have arrived; he said he lived outside the store, on the off chance he'd get a few hours paid. In the evening his missus brought him a tray of mollusks scraped from the side of boats in the harbor. I told him that trash was full of PCBs and other fun stuff, that you might as well chug a bucket of old engine oil. Laughed in my face."

"So what did you do?"

"My uncle's apartment is south facing. I made some window boxes outta these old plastic planks I found. Boosted some dirt from Prospect Park, back before it was a prison. I tried growing starches at first, potatoes, the stuff that keeps you alive, but those big rooftop farms sucked up that market, so I switched to luxury items, strawberries and blueberries. That did well enough to pay the rent."

"So why are you on the Bridge?"

"Winter. No sun. Need to save up and buy some UV lamps or we'll starve and—" He stopped. Alice could see Red wanted to say something, but after a long pause he just shook his head and changed the subject. "So how come you're a cop now?"

"My brother walked me into a drugs deal gone bad. He got death row on Rikers Island, I had the choice of that or the Marines."

"Not much of a choice."

"You say that, but there are times I think I made the wrong one. Did two years in the terrestrials, then two in the Colonials, one on Mars, one in rehab. After that there wasn't much else to do but police."

Red pulled an old black comb from his jacket and prodded his hair back into shape. "All right, I believe you. I have a midtown mail delivery. I tried skooching across on the ice. That didn't work, so decided to try the Bridge. Climbed a cable, fell, *boom*, we met."

"Worth risking your life for a letter?"

"Get off your throne, *officer*. Scorchers are supposed to look after each other, but you're only out for yourself, same as the rest of us."

Alice's fingers twitched with the urge to slap him for telling the truth. She inhaled and shook herself. "How were you planning to get to the island?"

"Dunno." Red stared at her, then dropped his gaze. "I didn't have much time to make a plan, okay?"

"When you were on the cable, did you see the Bridge layout? Somewhere high up we can get to?"

He looked up with an exhausted smile, face a hundred years old. "Yeah, yeah. I did, yeah." He shifted, pushed himself upright. "Right at the top there's this landing pad. It had this helicopter thing on it, chugging out black smoke. Pre-machine-phase stuff, had a long blade that spun round real fast like, cut yer head off if you jump. Fourth Warders were loading these cold boxes into it."

"How did you know they were cold?"

"'Cos they steamed frost. Fell like snow."

"What was in them?"

He shrugged. "Hell I know. Wasn't hanging around up there for intel.

They were taking real care though, like they'd be strung from the cables if they dropped them. Anyways, the pad was near these long greenhouses. They were lit super bright. I saw plants in there, fields like, of sunflowers."

"What?"

"Bank's symbol."

"I've no idea what you're talking about." Red looked at her with such an expression of contempt and exasperation that Alice dropped her gaze. "Cops don't come in here that much," she finished with a lame shrug.

"Yeah, Scorchers got a black eye and bugged out, typical. Sunflowers are Bank's sigil. You see that, you know to keep clear. He has thousands of 'em up there. We get to those, we could run our ways across to the other side."

"You're not running anywhere, Red. Like I promised, I'm getting you a ride out of here."

"I'm delivering this letter, don't try to stop me."

"I won't, but I can't do this and babysit you at the same time. Show me the roof and I'll call you a cab. After that I'll get intel and call in backup. Maybe they can use the landing pad you saw."

"Shit, your plan's as bad as mine."

"Maybe our paths converge, maybe not, but will you take my lead or will you bug first chance you get?"

Alice watched him think, run through the options. He was smart, which might keep him alive.

"Okay, sure," he said.

"Good. Suit, any suggestions?"

"I was wondering when you'd get around to me," the small speaker said. "I'm not just along for the ride, you know, I'm actively involved in this."

"So then actively involve yourself in looking for a way to the upper levels."

"May I suggest climbing every ladder you see? Why I constantly need to point out the obvious is beyond me."

Alice was about to reply when she saw Red's puzzled expression. "What?"

"You let it talk to you like that?"

"You're welcome to search for its warm and sunny side. Me? I haven't patience to cuddle up to a piece of clothing."

"Well, really," Suit grumbled.

Red grinned, a young, innocent look that made her smile back. There was a moment of silence between them, less awkward and adversarial.

"Time to go," she said, her voice quiet. The truth sat unspoken between them: there was no way Fourth Ward would let her walk off the Bridge. After today's action, Mr. Bank would make putting her head on a stick his number one priority. "That letter won't deliver itself, kid."

[16]

"The Turing threshold has been surpassed by the modern Mechanical Intelligence, but lesser 'smart-systems' can also appear sentient in the right context. In certain symbiotic relations—such as the military or police—they should be awarded the same rights as the wearer."
"The Nicholson Paper" on rights due to non-Turing smart-systems, presented to UN delegates, 2055

"My jacket? I hate my jacket. It's an asshole and there's a no-returns policy at the store. Typical."
NYPD officer Alice Yu, New York, 2055

Alice wiped her brow. The further they forced themselves along the maintenance corridor, the more it filled with equipment. Welded metal pipes formed organic clusters too hot to touch; smart cabling beeped data codes as they inched past. There was an underlying logic to the construction that reminded her once again of the repurposed NASA ship that ferried her to Mars.

She'd understood that ship, its bootstrapped weapons and life-support systems. Here, something was out of context. The Bridge had a haphazard external appearance, a mechanical accretion driven by short-term needs and wants. The inside was different: organized, planned, meticulous. Something here had prodigious power and data demands. The NYPD's Grand Central MI required sustenance at this level, but sentient machines cost more than skyscrapers, their locations strictly controlled by the UN. Analytical engines were, rightly, regarded as weapons of mass destruction. Misused they could destabilize the world's political and financial systems, and were afforded oversight with great care. Was there an illegal MI here? If so, how was that even possible?

Alice turned to Red, his pale face pinched and nervous in the gloom. "Time to see where we are," she said.

He nodded in reply as sweat dripped from his chin.

Alice clicked a toggle on her lapel and microdisplays lit up to scroll *NYPD* across her chest. The vivid white text pushed the dark away, reflected letters crawling along the worn metal ductwork.

"Subtle," Red said. "Can you change the lettering at least?"

Alice didn't have to do anything, Suit switching it to *Mama Pajama's Tequila Shack* as they looked at each other.

"Thanks, Suit, big help," she said.

"Don't look at me, you're the one that goes there every Friday night," it replied.

"You go *there*? You're sadder than I thought," Red said.

"Hey, I like tequila."

Suit gave a quiet chirp and Alice looked at Red, putting a finger to her lips.

They waited in silence, breath echoing from the damp, curved walls.

"Tactical," Alice whispered.

"I'm detecting rhythmic vibrations in the surrounding metal, ahead and behind," Suit said.

"Direction."

"Converging on our current location."

"Speed?"

"Forward vibrations have paused; rear have accelerated. Impact frequency suggests something heavy and slow."

"Trying to force us into an ambush?"

"Such an obvious outcome it didn't need saying."

Alice looked back the way they had come. The narrow space glistened in the damp. Had they passed any other exits? None. They'd taken every vertical route they found, each one more choked with cabling, power relays, and data-collation boxes than the last. She was lost now. Before Fourth Ward you could walk across the Bridge in thirty minutes, but crawling though these tunnels was slow and exhausting.

"Red, we've got to move and fast. Keep up."

She set off, forcing herself along. The space pressed inward, the weight of the structure a physical presence, the scents of hot steel and antifreeze heavy in the dampness. Mars shimmered in her peripheral vision, the edge of panic following as she moved. She had no defenses against her past; the further the red planet receded, the more it remained alive in her mind. She'd tried to shed her memories, thought she had at times, but they returned again and again, waiting until she was asleep or tired and defenseless. Her heart kicked with an unsteady rhythm and sweat ran between her shoulder blades. She smelled herself, a thick animal scent that reeked of fear.

Alice had dominated her past though the simple technique of constant stimuli. Kept her work life filled with crazy hours and the riskiest of patrols, fear and adrenaline used to smother the past. Off duty she drank too much, fucked too much, fried her mind with recreational drugs; when the money ran out, she played chess for quarters in the local park.

Anything not to be alone.

She'd tried the veteran's center once, but it was full of broken people who wanted to relive the past, not forget it.

"Suck it up, Red, hurry."

"Yeah, yeah," he panted.

Martian veterans had twice the suicide rate of Earth's warfare survivors, and Alice understood why. There were no post-trauma aversion techniques that could overcome the knowledge they had destroyed mankind's last hope of a new start. Night after night, she awoke covered in sweat, shivering, the shreds of nightmares pulling at her. The dreams made her sick, forced to rewatch the virginal forests burn, the tunnel collapse, the bodies (*children*) in a circle.

Alice checked again. Red was there at her shoulder, face lined with dirt and sweat. She arrived at a junction, turned sideways, sucked her stomach in, and squeezed herself through. Red followed.

"Alice?" Suit said. Its politeness scared her more than any warning.

"Yes?"

"It's closing fast, twenty feet. Hurry, hurry."

She grabbed Red's arm and dragged him onward; the wet, hot air made her lungs wheeze, broken ribs flaring pain, and she tasted copper and burned rubber.

"Up," Red panted from behind.

A narrow ventilation grille rattled ten feet overhead and cool air flowed over Alice's face. She jumped up; her hands brushed the grille but couldn't hold on. She gestured at Red, then bent and cupped them.

"Get in."

Red didn't need a second invitation. He put one huge boot in Alice's hands and reached for the vent. It rattled as he shook it, but remained in place: four large hex bolts oozed green sealant at each corner.

"Down," Alice said and dropped him to the floor. She checked her pistol. The shrapnel rounds were designed for widespread organic damage, ricochet for distant deflections. Neither were perfect, but she chambered the shrapnels and aimed at the grille. "Cover your ears."

The boom crackled from the bare metal walls. The plastic shrapnel rounds splintered upon firing, and the far left bolt shuddered. She fired again, again, concentrating on the left-hand side until the grille sagged.

Six rounds left.

"Suit?" she said and boosted Red back up.

"Progress has slowed. My guess is the tight confines are proving a challenge."

Alice remained still, cocked her ears, and listened. There—something, a scraping. Way too close.

"Red, hurry." She tried to keep her voice calm but couldn't, urgency adding a hard edge to it.

With a squeal of metal Red tore away the grille and Alice lifted his head and shoulders into the duct.

"Got it," he said, his boots vanishing upward. There was a banging noise, a stream of cussing, then his pale face frowned down at her.

"There is a branch duct here. Tight, but we can—"

A shadow grew on the curved metal wall beside Alice.

"Too late, kid," she said.

ALICE TURNED to face the chest of the biggest hack-job she'd ever seen. At least seven feet tall, his shaved and tattooed head wedged against the duct's thin metal ceiling. A blue zip scar connected his head to a pale Caucasian neck, another scar connected his neck to a coffee brown torso. Two wider flesh welds joined the torso to long muscled arms, the left thinner, knuckles silver, while the right looked strong enough to buckle steel. A Colonial Marines tattoo glowed on his right bicep—similar to Alice's but newer, the ink white, the dates different. He wore standard army pants, thick canvas with adaptive camouflage. As she watched, they blurred to mimic the wall behind. Black combat boots completed the street-punk ensemble.

Alice spent a year in rehab after Mars—half on the way back, half on Earth, her damage as much mental as physical. During the return flight a combat psychiatrist proposed getting her scanned and reprinted. He said a new body would skip the months of rehab she needed, saving further emotional trauma. Then a United Nations Organized Crime team arrived. Turned out most of the ship's doctors were owned by the Russian mob. They were scanning Marines—the truly messed up dead-heads—and using their recordings as part of print-to-order kill teams.

The man in front of her was a product of a similar process. He was a Klichka, a construct built from the best spare parts available. Not subtle, not able to hide in a crowd and kill with a knife, Klichkas were the blunt-force approach to modern warfare. Cheap, reliable, disposable.

The man forced himself past the power conduit, lights flickering. Alice went for her gun, her draw oil smooth, pistol up in a perfect arc until she sighted on his torso. The weapon kicked, and the man's chest sparkled with damage, but it was like throwing rice at an elephant. Thick green gel oozed from the cuts as he smiled at her with pointed white teeth.

Alice ejected the empty clip and stepped backward, fumbling for the ricochet cartridge. The hack-job forced himself toward her. She didn't have time to get a defensive block up, and he punched her in the middle of her chest. The blow was like an exploding grenade; air blew out of her as she flew backward, arms out, trying to keep her balance. Her boot caught a loose cable and the floor and ceiling swapped places. The impact was hard, breath forced from her in a scream. Hands against the cold floor, she tried to push up, her boots scrambling for friction.

The Klichka loomed over her, his huge body creaking forward like a rusted piece of industrial equipment. A fist grabbed Alice's jacket and lifted her to his eye level, boots two feet clear of the floor.

Alice slumped in his grip, eyes closed, then brought her right arm up and around in a perfect blow. She put everything she had into it, angled her body weight, shifted back so his chin was at arm's length. Her fist exploded in pain as his head shuddered. He smiled, teeth bloody, then slapped her face.

Her head rocked back, vision sparkling with pain, neck rubbery and loose. She didn't have time to pull herself upright before he slapped her again, on the other cheek, her head snapping the other way. Blood and grit filled her mouth, ears whining, skull throbbing.

She laughed, a bloodied gurgle that made the Klichka smile. With the ease of a hydraulic press he lifted and squashed her against the ceiling. The air was driven from her lungs, she couldn't breathe, vision fading in and out.

"You be so lucky fellow officer want you not dead." His voice was light and effeminate, with an odd accent, like Russian garbled by a broken translator.

Fellow officer? Did he mean Mike?

"Hey boyfriend," Alice said, voice slurred, "I don't need any favors." She made her fingers into a point and drove them into his eye. She'd meant to blind him, but the blow was too weak; he shouted, staggered backward and tossed her away, hand to his face.

Alice tried to control her fall, but was too battered to know which way was up; she landed on her side beneath the open air duct. She rolled onto her back, attempted to drag air into her lungs, find some last shred of energy. The floor shook; the killer was returning, and this time he wouldn't follow orders. Alice scrabbled backward, boots slipping across the oily floor. She looked up, hoping that Red had been smart and fled.

He hadn't. His pale face glimmered back at her from the vent. He was doing something, the white text from his jacket visible, then obscured by a bunch of cables. There was a blue flash, then the Klichka blocked her view, his mouth a thin line. His right eye was shut, purple swelling obscuring the pupil. He would kill her now, apologize later. Alice still had the knife in her left arm scabbard; if he got close, she—

Then the Russian was jittering out of control, body spasming, the stench of seared meat filling the duct. Blue electrical fire arced between the walls, as the red emergency lights exploded like firecrackers. The Klichka gave a gargled choke and fell onto Alice, torso shuddering.

"Hey Alice," Red shouted. "You okay?"

The Klichka weighed a half ton, and she couldn't breathe, her chest throbbing with the pain of his weight on her bruised and broken body. She tried to push him off, failed. She looked past his bulk to see Red haul up a thick black cable, sparks hissing from its torn end; he'd dropped it onto the hack-job's naked torso. Alice's jacket had saved her, its spider-silk layers nonconductive. Suit had crashed, its embedded lights flickering a digital snow storm.

There was one final bitter arc of light, a bang, then complete darkness. The reek of cordite made Alice gag as she spat blood onto the floor.

"Suit?" she gasped, hoping it could provide illumination, but only strangled feedback came from the collar speaker.

The floor shuddered as Red dropped from the vent and kneeled with a grunt to rock the huge body sideways. After a few attempts, Alice slid free.

In the pitch dark she grabbed his hand. Her legs shook. All she could hear was Red's panicked breathing and the thump of her heart.

It was hotter in the duct than before, the air tropical.

"Red, the conduit—is it big enough for me to fit through?"

"It's tight at first, doglegs right and opens up. I didn't go in very far."

"What did you do?"

"There's a bunch of power relays up there. My boots are rubber so I squeezed past, then kicked a cable free. Looks like it blew whatever grid ran through here."

"You know this stuff, huh?"

His thin shoulders shrugged.

"You did real good, Red. Now I'm going to boost you back up, okay?"

Alice's head throbbed as she stood, then lifted Red into the duct. She used the Klichka's hard torso as a step, found the lip of the opening, and followed him inside.

RED WAS PARTIALLY CORRECT, the duct widened out, but only enough to allow her to inch along, shoulders wedged against the tight steel confines, Red's shoes in front of her face. The walls glimmered with a faint light. The metal creaked and flexed with every movement, breath echoing from the walls.

Paralyzing claustrophobia lurked, but the primal instinct to survive held it off while years of training kept her moving. That and Red. He was just a street kid, like any of the thousands she ignored every day but, accident or not, he'd saved her life and she owed him.

Her suit crackled as a systems crash flashed interference patterns across its surface lights. It sparked blue, went dark. "What happened?" it said after a moment.

"We're in a duct," Alice said.

"Thank you for clarifying such painfully obvious details."

"You're welcome. How are you feeling?"

"Like I've been electrocuted."

"Specifics?"

"Some core component damage, battery depletion, and general need for a vacation."

"Well, I'm glad you're back."

"Thank you, Alice."

"Any tracking intel on the second target you picked up?"

"None. It seems your friend with the high-voltage cable has melted some of my sensors. I feel like your face looks. Lighting, however, is something I can provide." The spider silk glowed a soft red, enough so they could see without harming their night vision.

A moment later Suit said, "That's interesting."

"Suit—less theatrics. Just tell me." Alice inched her way forward. The air was stifling now, sweat dripping into her eyes. Unable to wipe it away, she shook her head, then winced as her bruised face throbbed.

"There is a large amount of internal radio chatter. Not wide band but localized. It's encrypted, of course, but some people are using older walkie-talkies with low-level capabilities, and I've hacked those. It seems Red's fun with the power conduit has caused quite the stink. There have been reports of cascading power outages to a lot of the cooling systems."

"That explains the heat," Alice said.

"Quite. Mr. Bank is rather upset; he's taken a personal interest in you."

"Awesome. How close are we to Mike?"

"Are you paying attention? I lost the ability to trace him when I was electrocuted."

"Hey, do you feel that?" Red said and stopped.

Alice was too slow and bumped into his boots. She tasted fresh blood in her mouth. "What?"

Then she felt it: a rhythmic vibration in the walls. With every passing second it intensified, stopped, then intensified again, the rhythm accelerating.

"Red, something's coming up behind. You've got to speed up."

"Okay."

"I mean it, Red. Go, now, hurry."

He moved, but not much faster than before. Alice struggled to follow, breath hitching in her chest. Screams rose in her, she wanted to shout at Red, kick him, anything to speed him up.

The vibrations grew.

"Suit?" she said.

"Hard to tell. The pattern suggests a human approach, but it's moving at a velocity far in excess of a biological entity."

"Roid?"

"I very much doubt Fourth Ward have any androids able to fit into this duct and chase you down. That would require a spec system, and it's far cheaper to use reprints. No, this is something I haven't seen before."

Alice stopped and tried to look back by raising her torso and bending her head down. At first there was nothing, then thirty feet behind her blinked two points of light. Eyes, looking at her.

She redoubled her efforts, gave up on politeness and shoved Red forward, arms and legs squashed together, haunted by the chasing vibrations.

Closer, closer.

Red shouted and Alice realized she could see at last, Suit's glow overwhelmed by a dull gray wash. Red was pulling at a grille in the floor.

He looked up at her, eyes white with fear. "It's stuck," he cried, beating his hands against it.

Then he was gone, falling through head first. Alice didn't pause to see what was below, just grabbed the edge of the grille and pulled herself out and down.

She landed on a hard concrete floor, rolled, and came up in a crouch. Stark white walls glowed beneath radiation markers and environmental graphics. Red lay spread-eagled near her, rubbing his head. Alice caught his collar and dragged him away from the opening, at the same time fumbling for her sidearm.

They were halfway along the corridor when something exploded from the duct, moving so fast it was hard to track. It looked part human, part machine, and moved with oiled precision. Alice fired from the hip, the shots wide, the creature too fast. She dropped Red and took aim: no good. It skipped from the floor to the walls, sparks tracking its progress.

"Suit, *help*," she screamed and slapped in her last clip of ricochet rounds.

"Firing solutions," Suit shouted and projected a series of red lights onto the wall.

Alice aimed at the closest; the creature was almost upon her, its blur vibrating in her peripheral vision. She fired as fast as she could, emptying the clip in seconds, then drew her knife, the last weapon she had.

The composite rounds bounced across the corridor to hit the creature with a cloud of projectiles. Sparks flared like fireflies from its head; it roared and powered forward, but the ricochets had damaged it somehow. As Alice ducked left, it couldn't follow, barreling straight past her. She slashed out with her knife, the white fractal blade slicing deep. There was the odor of engine oil and dirt as thick green liquid arced over the opposite wall. The knife caught on something and the blade snapped with a dry *crack* that wrenched her sideways.

The creature flew past to collide headfirst with the far wall. It screamed and Alice realized this was another Klichka variant, a woman, more machine than the earlier version, body mutated into a human pit bull. The woman jerked, out of control, feet slapping the floor, arms pounding the wall. The crescendo grew, panels buckling to reveal more knotted black cabling.

"Alice, do something," Red shouted.

The Klichka blew, some overloaded central battery releasing a grenade-level explosion. Alice was tossed backward, the shockwave rolling over her like a steam train. A blizzard of orange sparks set fire to the rubber floor, the material sizzling as it poured smoke into the space. She tried to move but her body was offline; nothing worked. The smoldering wall belched gray clouds that filled the corridor with choking bitterness. More conduits popped in a deafening sequence that ran toward her.

"The power circuits are fried," Red screamed at her. "It's falling over, one relay at a time." He crawled across, grabbed the front of her jacket, and pulled. He was shouting, louder, but his words were lost in the maelstrom.

With a groan Alice rolled onto her knees and followed him along the corridor, past the dead woman, and through a circular steel door. Thick metal clanged behind them, and the roar fell away, leaving a brittle silence broken only by their gasped breaths.

"Well, this is turning out to be quite the day," Suit said.

ALICE LAY against the curved wall and watched Red strip a wire from an overhead conduit.

"Gonna run power to the door, let anyone the other side get a nice shock," he said.

"Learned all this from protecting your window garden, huh?"

"Either that or go to school."

"You make a compelling argument." She tried to smile, but her mouth hurt too much.

"Can you move?" Red said.

The stim inhaler had worn off long ago, leaving her body to deal with its chemical aftershocks. The worst pain came from her ribcage; something had happened when the Klichka collapsed onto her. She didn't have a punctured lung, but her insides shifted, loose and wet. Her jaw and legs throbbed, but that was superficial damage. She pushed herself upright.

"Help me." She held out her arm. Red slipped it across his thin shoulders and lifted.

"Suit, any suggestions?"

"Give up while you still can."

"Helpful."

She looked around. The corridor ran twenty feet to another submarine door. It was hot in here now, stifling. She chewed her lip as the overhead lights sparked. The floor shook with distant explosions; electrical systems popped like firecrackers on the other side of the door.

Suit was right, its sociopathic intelligence arrowing to the truth—she didn't know how to find Mike, and was in no shape to rescue him even if she did. For a moment Alice closed her eyes and savored the thought of surrender. They would kill her, of course, and that beautiful velvety blackness beckoned to her: so close, so absolute, so peaceful. She'd been smothered by that blanket once before, and had raged against the medics and machines who brought her back.

Isn't that what you want?

The thought came out of nowhere, yet it felt so at home, so much a part of her, that she couldn't ignore it. After Mars, no street patrol had been too risky, no arrest too dangerous. She'd led the chase into the alley that brought them here. A memory came back to her, of Mike shouting for her to stop, that the dead end was too dangerous.

She'd ignored him because—

No.

Yes.

The realization felt like a dam breaking, the knowledge flooding her mind, death's dark appeal laid bare yet reduced of its potency. Alice let her emotions churn. Her selfish desire to find a way out, *any* way, had brought harm to the very people she should have been protecting. Mike's capture was her fault, no one else's, and carrying on with Red was piling error upon error. He had to be her priority now—getting him out and nothing else. It was time to stop, run, and get help.

"Red," she said. "We're heading straight up and out. I'll come with you the whole way."

"What about your partner?"

"I can't save him and if you—we—go in further, none of us will survive. Once we're safe I'll call the shift sergeant and tell them face to face. See if they can swing a SWAT team to come here. If my credit stretches I can buy some extra help as well."

"Official backup is highly unlikely without new evidence," Suit said. "You leave now, Officer Squire will die in here."

"We don't know that for sure. I was only thinking of myself, following him in here. That's one thing I can change today."

Alice stood and set off, struggling to ignore the doubts and insecurities that hovered over her.

[17]

"The current operations are a suitable testing ground for smart munitions. However, we cannot ignore budgetary constraints: the human element is by far the cheapest and most easily replaced of modern combat componentry."
Pentagon Report, "War in the Age of Sentient Machines,"
President of the United States, 2053

———

"End of the day, it all comes back to politics. War, employment, death —everything."
Corporal McKinney, Martian occupation force, Mars, 2054

———

RED FOLLOWED ALICE, DEEP IN THOUGHT. IF HE'D MET HER ON the streets, he would have said she was in control, safe and secure in her brotherhood of police. Now that he knew her, she seemed flinty, brittle, as if one sharp blow would shatter her to a thousand pieces.

He recognized that mixture of fear and panic, having seen it in his mother. Whereas Alice still functioned, it had poisoned his mom, and leeched out to corrupt everything she touched. Red slowed to a standstill, realizing his mother had never said she would come home again. When was the last time he'd even seen her, anyway?

It had been on the Boatel, the Hudson's floating detention center. His mom was in for some bullshit charge, and had called Red to get her out. The ship was tethered to the George Washington Bridge, a long funicular railway ferrying jeeks in and out the holding cells.

She waited for him at the entrance as he used his few remaining dollars for bail. Afterward, they sat on the side of the river, the turbulent water somehow producing a moment of peace between them. Red begged her to come back, but she said little in return, just closed her eyes and listened to the waves.

In the end she'd stood, kissed his cheek, wiped his face with the edge of her shirt, turned, and walked away. He'd held it together until he made it home, then cried for so long that his uncle joined him on the sofa to cradle him as if he were a baby.

Red took out the letter. This morning it had been pure, untouched. Now it was wet, filthy, ruined. He looked at Alice as she moved along the corridor. Wasn't this what he wanted? She could get him out, even said she'd stick him in a Hopper, fly him to Cortex to hand deliver the message. He turned it over to see that the Professor's wax sigil was still in place. It was worth five dollars, nothing more. Most likely Mom would take the cash and disappear again.

And what of his uncle? The old man had asked nothing of him, only taken delight in his presence. What would happen if Red moved out?

This Scorcher, this cop, this *woman* could save him, if he trusted her.

"You going to keep up or just lounge there with your mouth open?" Alice said.

Red jumped, reverie broken, to see her watching him. He looked at the envelope.

"It's only a letter," he said under his breath.

"You've changed your tune. A few hours ago that was life or death."

"It was. It is. But ..."

"What?"

"I don't know what matters anymore. My plan was to earn some money and use it to get my mom back. That's the point of this, not to buy Dust or clothes."

"I'm sorry, Red, I didn't know."

"But maybe she won't. Come back, I mean. She never said she would. Maybe she's like you."

"I'm not following."

"Don't get me wrong, I appreciate your help. I'd be dead left to myself. But, you know, bailing on your friend is cold. Maybe Mom's the same, just says stuff 'cos it's easy, but in the end she only looks after herself." Red gasped, words out of his mouth before he could stop them. "Sorry, sorry, but, you know what I mean."

"That's not what I'm doing here, Red."

"Yeah, but isn't it, though? You're abandoning your friend to whatever fate Bank has in mind. That's cold, right there ..." His voice trailed off as she stared at him.

"I'm not abandoning him, I'm saving you."

"I don't want that guilt. I want to go get him."

"We'll die down here if we go after him. I can accept that fate, but I'm not letting it happen to you." Alice took her jacket off and examined an array of purple bruises. Her arms were thin, strong, tanned. High up on the right one was a tattoo, a red sphere with the letters *USCM* across it. He'd seen it before: his uncle had the earthbound version.

"You were in the Colonials?" he said, desperate to change the subject.

She nodded, head down.

"Mars? Saw action?"

She raised her head, lips a white line.

"Come on, we need to go," she said.

"That's why you hate the tunnels, ain't it? 'Cos they remind you of up there." He nodded at the ceiling.

She walked over to him, her face gray and hard. She stopped an inch from his chest, her presence a mixture of exhaustion, soot, and musky perfume. The air grew warm until Red was shedding sweat into his jacket, heart hammering. He didn't know if she would beat him or leave him.

"You don't get to talk about that." She raised a fist, skin white around her clenched knuckles.

"Officer Yu, pull yourself together," Suit said from its location on the floor behind her.

She stared at Red, anger boiling from her. Then it was gone in an instant. She sagged backward, turned, and picked up Suit. "Keep slowing us down, kid, we'll both end up hating tunnels or worse."

AFTER THAT SHE wouldn't listen whenever he tried to start a conversation, just telling him to shut up. They worked their way upward for a grueling hour before slumping to an exhausted halt. The duct was dripping water from broken condensers, the air thick with heat and mildew. Red kept his leather jacket on—he never took it off except to sleep and wash—but Alice removed hers.

This time he got a better view of her tattoo. The circle wasn't Mars; it was the symbol of the Martian Parliament building. Even Red knew that mission had been fucked from the start.

"Tell me what happened," he said.

"No."

"It's time you told someone, Alice," Suit said. "You can't carry on like this."

She didn't look up, just rubbed her arm and closed her eyes. "No."

"If not now, when?" Suit said.

"I'm not debating this with a smart-system."

"How about debating it with me?" Red said.

"I don't want to talk about it."

"Would telling me be that bad? You could spend your last few hours alive not hating yourself so much."

"For a street kid, you're annoyingly observant."

"I saw some pictures of the domes, the early models, made out of them gel pillows."

"That was to suck up radiation. They yellowed with the dosage, so you could see which ones needed replacing."

"I thought they spent most of their time underground."

Alice took a deep breath and continued. "That was later. At the start the Martian settlers based their habitat designs on the lunar series: circular biomes connected by curved corridors radiating outward. Half above and half below ground, hence their Moles nickname. The colonists traveled on those big Space X shuttles, the ones with the bulb tips. We understood why they did it. There wasn't such a divide between Earth and Mars back then."

"I never got why they sent you."

"Mechanical Intelligence's caught them out, same as the rest of us. Think about it: the X shuttles take six to nine months to get there; a radio signal can upload a body scan in minutes. China got a printer there first, must have hidden it on a supply run. Soon they were adding hundreds of reprints to the population, which meant they won every vote. Mars had been this self-regulating colony, but as the demographics tilted, democracy slipped away. Mars was under UN jurisdiction—being the first multination off-world settlement—so the initial colonists asked them to intervene. The UN ordered China to stop, but they refused, said their scientists formed a nation-state province outside Earth control."

"So the UN sent you in to take over?"

"Not at first, but there was too much at stake for either side to back down. The UN formed the Colonial Marines as a deterrent, I think, made of soldiers from every member country. I'm not sure we were ever supposed to be deployed, but once you have a weapon it's oh-so tempting to use it. After a year of political stalemate the Moles acted for themselves and killed the reprints. That forced the UN's hand; they bought a Jupiter Mission ship from NASA, retrofitted it for the military. We were directed to reestablish Earth-based control, which was the polite way of saying kill everyone who refused to surrender. You know, stick a flag in the Martian soil, claim it for the starving and hopeless back home."

"But it didn't work like that."

Alice laughed, the cold bark echoing around the damp metal surroundings. "Got that right, kid. The UN thought it would be your standard asymmetrical engagement: go in heavy, shock them into surrender."

"What happened?"

"It took a year to retrofit the *Fucker* and get us up there. By the time we arrived they'd turned the buildings into threshing machines. Marines went in, blood came out."

"You?"

"I missed something I shouldn't have and a lot of people died."

"Was it your fault, though? Them Moles sound pretty smart."

The words hung between them. She didn't reply, just stared at the wall in front of her, unblinking.

"It wasn't like that," she said.

And then she told him.

MARTIAN INDEPENDENT REPUBLIC, 2052

THE PARLIAMENT DOME was built from three interlocking foil layers. Each was perforated in such a way as to create dappled shadows in the debating chamber below. They moved on separate tracks like a huge clock; every minute the mechanism gave a dry *click* as it shifted.

If the mission brief had been correct—and military intelligence had to get *something* right today—even if by sheer luck, the entrance would be less than a hundred feet away. Alice looked up; the black rain had stopped, the lake and steam gone, but the burning forest still blazed around her. The air stank of the fires, her mouth coated with a gritty texture. Her lungs were working hard, and every few steps she had to stop and gulp like a beached fish. The MI had calculated how long the trees would burn, and how much oxygen that would take. It had been wrong, or perhaps the crack in the foundation had opened the dome up to some underground pollutants. The atmosphere was becoming unbreathable.

Alice pulled a filter over her face, its carbon-black weave cutting out the stench of smoke. It would block particulates, but she didn't have an oxygen pack that could help.

She kept moving and soon saw the building's entrance ahead, the white concrete ring beam cut away to reveal the lip of a red stone crater.

Alice stopped, the surrounding horror gone for a moment. It had been twelve minutes since the *It's Been A Long Week* began its drop, and she hadn't had a minute to consider that she was on Mars, on another planet. She crouched, eyes closed, and put her hand on the floor. Below her, past all the human shit, were soil and microbes and water and fossils from an alien world.

"Marine, are you injured?"

A hand cupped her elbow; it was Gallagher, a field medic. He looked worse than Alice felt, the side of his face blackened, teeth missing. Two stim patches nuzzled against his neck and his pupils were like saucers. Still, he was here, alive. The desire to babble platitudes, to hug him, was so strong Alice had to push him away, breathe deep, act like a goddam Marine for once.

"No sir, minor injuries. I'm the only survivor of the *Long Week*, though."

"It's been a bad morning all round. We're over here, at the assembly point."

She followed, her strides light in the reduced gravity, to reach a huddle of Marines about to breach the building. A tech was working at the door controls, tablet open and jacked in. Green code scrolled across its screen.

"How many?" Alice said.

"With you, twenty-three out of the sixty. The *Why Can't We Just Get Along?* made it down before they set the bomb off. The *Mess* and *Long Week* went down hard. You're the only one walking out of those two. Nine from the *Mess* are alive but in no shape to move."

"Any contact with the *Fucker?*"

"None. All comms are out. I've not seen a weapon like that before. Our gear was supposed to be shielded."

"First to go, last to know."

"Got that right."

"What's the plan?"

"Sergeant McNulty is leading us in. We're following mission parameters to secure the dome. After that is a judgement call. You okay?"

"Good to go."

"Get ready."

"Thee, two, one, now."

Alice was in the breach team. The hackers cracked the door code, and moved back as her four-person group broke in and spread out, followed by the rest.

They'd trained in Virts, so were prepped for the surroundings. Alice focused on checking for combatants, then IEDs, as she scuttled between the rows of seats. The Moles had been intelligent with their architecture, as in so many things. They'd left the ancient crater alone as much as possible, using its curved sides to support the rows of seats. A concrete floor and lectern had been added at the center for presentations. This was where they executed the UN envoy, the video broadcast worldwide.

Except the envoy was alive and sat on the floor, along with her four bodyguards. There was a *click* as the dome shifted, light flickering over their faces.

"It's about goddam time," the envoy shouted, her voice echoing from the hard surfaces. "They've gone down into the tunnels. Now get me out of here."

Alice ignored them, and worked with her team to make sure the chamber had been cleared. There were no weapons, traps, explosives, or Moles here. Nothing except five very much alive and pissed-off people in gray suits.

Alice took up perimeter security as McNulty spoke to the envoy, his rough Scottish accent carrying in the quiet.

"What happened here? We thought you were dead," he said.

"Dead? Why would we be dead? We relayed their demands. It was the UN that came back with unreasonable subclauses. I have a series of proposals for the security council, and need transport back to the ship. We've been radioing you, but never got a reply."

"You must be mistaken, ma'am," McNulty said. "We received no communications."

"I managed to work that out for myself once you blew the dome and made your dumb entrance. They went down there." She pointed to what looked like a maintenance hatch in the flat concrete floor.

"Ma'am, we have no direct comms to the ship, so can't get you out right now. We are going to proceed with our mission directives as ordered. You stay here; we will leave water and rations plus two Marines for support. The rest are going into the tunnels. If we can't get communications back up, the *Fucker* will nuke us in five hours. There has to be an off-world relay station somewhere down there that can get a message out."

―――――

"Sarge?" Alice said as she snatched a look backward. The tunnel curved away behind her, the radius far wider than that of the parliament building overhead. They'd been down here for an hour, edging further and further underground, the floor always leading downward. The dome's heat had been replaced with a frigid cold. Her breath fogged the air, her arms shivered.

The remnants of the Marines task force hunched back around the curve. Alice kneeled on one knee, undecided what to do next. The corridor ran straight ahead for a hundred feet to end in a heavy steel door. They'd passed through two of these already, but her back itched with fear.

After basic training Alice had been sent to the Texas wall. Half the time she worked as a sniper from the armored turrets, the other half was spent in the wilderness tracking down insurgents. Out there she had taken point duty more than any other Marine. Her sergeant even joked about it, said she was a telepath or some high-tech cyborg. It wasn't that. She'd spent years in the abattoir of New York City, honing her survival instincts to a keen edge, and had learned to trust her feelings. Now they were telling her something was off, she just didn't know what.

The corridor matched so much Martian architecture: ten-foot-tall sheets of armor glass formed curved walls, red soil visible on the other side. A flat, pink concrete floor reflected gel-pack lighting.

A low throb pulsed at the base of her skull, a dry thirst in her mouth. There was no sign of the Moles; it was as if they never existed. She pulled the hydration straw from her armor and sucked on the sickly red gel.

"Sarge?" she hissed again, faint echoes returning from the walls. *Goddam shit comms gear.* She rattled her helmet to no effect. Her headache had been building since she stopped, and it grew like a thundercloud to mock her indecision.

Then the corridor rippled as if underwater. She shook her head, sweat spinning away as silver dots in the air. The rippling stopped, if it had ever occurred.

A crackling sound filled her helmet, garbled noise from her headphones. She slapped the Kevlar shell with her palm. The rattle stilled; a voice came from behind.

"Yu, what's the delay?"

"There's something here, Sarge. Maybe. I'm not sure. Seeing things."

"Hold."

Alice crouched, sighted down the long barrel of her rifle, waited. McNulty crept up behind. He said nothing, didn't need to, just unhooked his dead visor and pulled out an old set of lensed binoculars. They ran different wavelength algorithms with a low whirr.

"Fatigue?" he said after a minute.

"I don't think so, sir. Perhaps. I don't know."

"I got nothing," he answered after a few seconds. "What you see?"

"The tunnel rippled, like water or oil. There, gone, then nothing."

"You've been on point for thirty. Time to swap out."

"No, I can do it."

"That wasn't a question. You're fatigued or in shock. I can't have you hallucinating on me. Step down."

"Sir."

Alice rose, knees popping in the quiet, and jogged back around the corner, high-fiving Phelps as he ran forward, then sat in a low crouch at the rear of the team. Being the point guard was exhausting beyond any physical exercise. Maybe Sarge was right, and she was in shock. Texas had been rough—she'd seen plenty of action—but nothing like that attack run. Her head throbbed, a dull ache that radiated from the base of her skull. It was rhythmic, hypnotic. She dragged herself upright, shook herself. She nudged Thomasson ahead of her, and he swung round with a goofy grin.

"We going or what?" she said.

He didn't reply, instead giving her the blissed-out look she recognized from nightclubs back home. But Thomasson was as antidrugs as the rest of the white-trash born-to-kill Christians he'd signed up with. Alice's headache spiked, sharp steel pins in her mind. The armor-glass wall opposite glowed with a red-blue halo. The scent of peppermint filled the air.

Alice's legs shook and gave out, throwing her face-first to the floor, rifle clattering away on the concrete. She twitched as nerves fired, but her muscles had seized like rusted farm equipment. She concentrated, forced herself onto her knees, the horizon rolling, gravity a lost concept. Thomasson lifted his head, burped a happy giggle, and stuck his thumbs in his eyes. As she watched, a scream locked inside her throat, he pulled them out and licked the bloody mess like lollypops.

Alice looked up to witness her platoon slicing themselves to shreds, some opening their stomachs with boot knives, others shooting themselves. Alice dragged herself on all fours around the bend to see Top lying unconscious on the floor. She raised her rifle in hands that shook so hard it was impossible to aim. Blue flames leaped from the barrel, the *brrrrrrppp* of the weapon drowning out the screams of her friends.

The tunnel rippled and came apart. The Moles had stretched nanocamouflage across the shaft, its weave mimicking the background perfectly. The sheet exploded under the gunfire to reveal a red cylinder attached to a wide nozzle. It hissed as it bled hallucinogenic gases into the air.

Blood flooded the floor beneath her. Her hands were claws, should she cut them off? A steel blade was there, in her arm sling. She pulled it free, the rainbow of its edge—

No.

With a shiver, she dropped the knife and staggered toward the cylinder. She made it, clung on. There was no way to shut it off; the gas was inside her now, soaking from her pores with the dazzling blue fire of a Dust trip. She fumbled at her belt for a thermal grenade, tore the firing pin free, and tossed it between her and her team. She tried to cover her head, failed. The grenade was still in her hand.

Or was it—

—there—

—why was, it was …

Fire filled her universe, flames smothering her, searching for every crack in her armor, the composite running like wax. Her hair was burning, skin black. The armor-glass wall folded inward like a wet cardboard tube to leave her in roaring, sealed blackness.

Alice awoke into a void defined by pain. Was she dead? She floated and struggled to remember where she was, who she was. Memories danced, fragments bursting like flames only to die away. The pain localized; her face was raw, her scalp radiating waves of agony that drowned out every other sensation.

A cold, hard floor pressed against her back. She was lying somewhere dark. She tried to move, but pain erupted in a storm so she stopped. There was an anesthetic stick in her belt. She waggled her fingers: they worked. She walked them across her belt, inch by inch, until they brushed the cold, hard tube. She flipped the cap in the dark, turned the cylinder around and jammed it into her stomach.

Burned skin shrieked, then a numb blanket smothered her, sensations nothing but distant voices. She floated.

A scrape in the dark, nails over stone. Again, closer. Something was in here with her, something that used the tunnels, that liked to trap people, to chew on bones like old wood. Peppermint—

That triggered her. Peppermint. Her team. Gas canisters. Paranoia. Fear.

She was in a Martian tunnel, tripping out of her gourd on hallucinogenic gas. Waves of claustrophobia crashed over her, and a crippling fear of the dark pummeled her senses. She knew it was false, had spent months living in New York's sewers, but that didn't help, the emotions too strong to fight.

She scrambled for her second anesthetic stick, jammed it into her elbow and embraced the blackness that blossomed to envelop her.

How LONG HAD she been out? When would the *Fucker* release its nukes? It couldn't be long; so much of this had happened out of sight of its surveillance systems. The pain medication was failing, spikes stabbing through her with every breath. If she was going to do anything, it had to be now.

Alice rolled to her side, gasped, pushed herself upright. There was nothing, just absolute dark. Her armor was deformed—hard and lumpen—making moving difficult. With desperate care she ran her hands over her body and peeled the main panels of her uniform away. Buckled and warped, they fell to the floor with a clatter. They'd saved her life: only her midriff was raw, where the panels were thinner. She checked her equipment. There was nothing left except her pistol and gel-pack light. She pulled the pack out, cracked its spine, and shook it until a pale glow grew bright enough for her to see.

The tunnel was no longer armor glass, but native red Martian stone. Drill bit marks from demolition charges marked every few feet. This had to be one of the earliest tunnels, dug back in the first few years. The floor was still flat concrete. Ten feet ahead lay a small blue glove with a unicorn logo. She raised the gel stick and gasped in pain as burned skin cracked. There was nothing else to be seen.

Alice limped forward, a cloud of fear overhead. Claustrophobia came close to crippling her, the feeling that at any second she'd be trapped here, unable to breathe, the weight of the ground above growing heavier, heavier.

The floor sloped ever downward. There were more signs of life now. A discarded toy, a half-eaten energy bar, some new shoes.

Her gel stick dimmed as the walls became rough-hewn stone. She ran her hands over them as she limped forward, touching rock from another world.

Terror came in surges. The tunnel, so cold and hard, filled with heat and humidity, as if she were sliding down the stinking gullet of some long-dead animal. Tentacles stroked her cheeks, grazed her ankles. She spun around, burned skin oozing blood, to see nothing but empty shaft passing out of sight. The fear faded, replaced by terrors of ancient things with hard scales and waxen skin beckoning her onward.

The anesthetic shots dwindled with every step. Her scalp hurt the most, a hot, raw sensation as if she were still on fire. A desire to stop and lay down fought with an inner voice that pushed her on. The voice was weak, though, coming and going, while the desire for rest grew relentlessly.

If she stopped now, there was no getting up.

The shaft ended at a heavy door with a central spin-wheel lock. The Rocket X logo was embossed in its steel, followed by *018,* the first ship to land on Mars. This had to be it, the original deep tunnel and habitat.

Alice reached for the handle, but then stopped herself. Was it a trap? They'd blown Marines out of the sky, burned them, poisoned them. Why would they leave this here, untouched?

"Fuck it," she said and grabbed the handle.

Nothing happened.

She spat blood on the floor, and rotated the lock counterclockwise. It moved, the mechanism oiled, and with a *snick* the door swung open. There was a brief gust of warm air, an odd scent, then more darkness.

"Hello?"

Silence. She stepped over the door's metal lip and into a white ceramic room. She held the gel stick up, its feeble light barely enough to pick out the interior of an airlock. There was an access panel beside the inner seal. She placed her hand against it and lights glowed to life. There was a background buzz of electricity, the *tink* of cooling metal, then the inside door unlocked.

Alice peered into this new room, its gray twilight revealing forms on the floor. She didn't want to go in, her fear amplified to terrifying heights by the drugs in her system.

"No," she said. She just wanted to stop, give up, sleep.

Her feet moved of their own accord, up and over the lip, into the room. It was circular and narrow, the metal walls and ceiling lit by wire-covered lights. A console bristling with equipment rose from the middle. A small green light blinked.

She looked at the floor.

The Moles were here. She'd found them at last, arrayed in a circle, ordered from old to young. The original settlers took the outside spaces, feet against the wall. Next were the second, then third crews: younger, heavier. Children made up the final ring, six corpses encircling the center console.

They had dressed for their deaths, clothes washed and pressed, hands crossed and holding sheets of paper. Alice kneeled beside an old woman and saw that the paper in her hands was a signed and authorized recycling form. They had remained scientists to the last, their bodies offered up to fertilize soil on the planet they considered their own.

Alice stepped over the woman, then a man, refusing to look at the children (—*blond hair, shoulder length; white skin, thin lips with—*) and reached the console. It was a bootstrapped communications panel from the settler's first ship. The blinking green light signaled an upload buffer; it contained a thirty-second video. Someone had taped a handwritten note to a small red button: *If you are a human first, a soldier second, send this with no regrets.*

Alice pressed the button. It was old, mechanical. It clicked and released the signal, some remote colony transmitter sending whatever the Moles had wanted to say. She waited until the transmission was complete, then raised a microphone to her scorched lips.

"Mars is taken," she said, then sat in the dim light and let the terrors in.

NEW YORK, 2055

"So THAT's where their last video came from. I never knew. It was a big deal down here, new laws and everything 'cos of that. Did they ever find who sent the fake one? With the UN envoy losing her head?" Red said, his surroundings and predicament momentarily forgotten.

"No. A Mars relay was hacked. Rumor has it some rogue MI did it, but they could never prove anything. The whole raid was based upon a lie."

"But you didn't know that."

"No."

"And the deal with the gas, how were you to know? That landing would have screwed anybody up."

"I knew something was there. I didn't hold my ground."

"You were ordered to quit, though. It don't sound so bad to me."

Alice sat opposite him, her heavy boots pulled in tight, knees to her chest, arms wrapped like a shield. She lifted her head and stared at him, lips back in a snarl. "*What?*"

"You're saying the mission was based on a faked video, right, and you missed some super-secret high-tech camouflage thing, and everyone died. That's no big bad on you."

"You don't get it, kid. They died because I fucked up. It's my fault."

"No it ain't. You were out of your depth, right? They should have sent a drone in or something, but were too cheap for any of that high-tech stuff. Soldiers cost nothing these days, what with the unemployment. Everyone knows that. Look, I ain't saying you're a hero or anything, but you got to get a grip."

She stared at him, silent, black eyes unblinking.

"I'm right, aren't I?" Red pressed. He knew it was dumb to say more, but he couldn't stop himself, the words tumbling out. "All that anger you're carrying is old news. You need to give it up."

"I spent a year in rehab. First on the ship back, then down here."

Alice scratched her scalp with a dirty finger. "This is all new, the hair, the skin, my face. Got the tags if you shave me. The reprint grafts hurt, but they had drugs to fix that. This was harder." She tapped her skull.

"That why you joined police instead of some plush tower-security gig?"

"Yeah. There are too many memories in my head. Do anything chill and I start thinking about it, over and over in a loop I can't stop. If I keep busy they stay out of the way."

"Killing yourself won't fix anything."

"The Moles poisoned their kids because of us. I can't shake that, or accept it. Every time I sleep I see them. Younger than you: six, four. Their clothes—" She stopped, unable to continue.

"Driving yourself into the recycling vats won't bring them back. Last thing I expected from you was cowardice."

"What are you talking about?"

"Putting a gun to your head is hard, yeah? Takes guts to do that and pull the trigger. But making it so someone else does it to you is a cheat's way out. This death-wish stuff puts your team, your partner, straight in the firing line, right?"

"*Always faithful*"—Alice didn't sound bitter to Red, just tired and scared—"is the Marines motto."

"See what I mean? What's the cop one? *To protect and serve?* Does that mean anything to you, or they just slogans on badges you wear?"

"They used to mean something." Fatigue cut deep creases in her face that grew as she looked at him. "But I'm not so sure anymore."

"Marines, cops, your job is to protect those who can't protect themselves. Killing yourself rejects that code." Red pulled out the letter again, filthy and wet. It dripped water onto the floor. "This letter is bullshit, I understand that now. Some things you just have to accept, no matter how bitter. But you can't go back, ever. Done is done. You're in the here and now, get that? You and me. We're the good guys, and good guys don't leave their friends behind. You got to put him first, over us." Red stopped, his breathing heavy.

"If we try to get Mike, we'll die."

"Some partner you are."

"I came here to save my job, just as much as save him."

"That make you feel good?"

"Fuck no," she said with a quiet laugh.

"The Marines in the drop-ship …" Red said.

"Careful."

"You leave them there? Or you go back when you could?"

"I know what you're saying, but this is different."

"No it ain't. Your Scorcher partner? I don't give two shits what he's done, all I know is he's scared and alone, just like us. Think you have it tough? Look at me. Every day I choose the hard option. I could run drugs, be so easy. Lots of money, life expectancy all fucked up for sure, but living large, short term. Or I could go to one of them big unemployment halls, get my red gel pack and watch the screens. But I ain't gonna do that, I *ain't*. This is us, right here. I say who I am, not some stupid-ass job. Can't you see that?"

Alice searched her jacket pockets, ignoring him.

"You know what I'm saying is right, I see you do. Stop being so selfish and let's go get him."

"What is he to you? Why do you care so much?"

Red leaned against the wall, its thin metal bowing outward. The light was dim, the dank air hot. "I care 'cos he's one of us. If we're not in this together, if we can't rely upon our friends, then we're screwed."

Alice took an electric cigarette from her jacket, stuck it in her mouth. She toggled it twice but it refused to light.

"Do you actually need reminding that you've exceeded this month's nicotine allowance?" Suit said. "It's another seven days until month's end. One more week and you can re-up." It paused. "I'm sorry, Alice. I can't break my programming."

She looked at the cigarette and tossed it away. "They took him for a reason, Red. No way Bank's picking up cops for fun."

"Yeah, so?"

"So? I could spring him, then end up arresting him straight after."

"What d'you think he'd prefer? Mars is nothing but guilt to you now—guilt you made it out, and they didn't. Do you really need more? It wasn't your fault. You gotta let it go."

Alice looked at him with an expression of such utter loss that tears filled his eyes. He moved over until their arms pressed together, and took her hand. She gripped his tight.

"You have to understand the situation, Red. I will do anything I can to protect you, but there are limits. We go on and ..."

He nodded, mouth dry. "This isn't on you. If I die, it's my choice."

"What do you think, Suit?" Alice said.

"It's time to stop running. The boy is right. We're here, so let's make it count. Tomorrow will take care of itself."

"You know the odds."

"Better than you. We started this together. Let's finish it that way."

Alice looked at the floor for so long Red thought she'd passed out, but then she pushed herself upright, wiped her hands on her jeans, and stared at him.

"If we're doing this, then let's do it right. It's time to meet Mr. Bank."

[18]

"A job for life was a viable notion for only a few years. After that, it was the corporations who dictated longevity. It always puzzled me why people were so loyal to monoliths that cared so little for them. Much better to get out there and enjoy the freedoms we are about to give you."
Robin Liar, CEO of Bensla Construction Inc., while announcing 67% job cuts across the firm, 2048

―――

"It is imperative we outlaw augmented human design. First, there is no need; humans and Mechanical Intelligences are more than capable of ruling. Second, why would we willingly create our evolutionary superiors? Do we hate ourselves so much we strive for our own extinction?"
UN Secretary General, G15 Council speech after establishing both D-PRO (Department Of Proliferation Control) and D-SIS (Department of Synthetic Intelligence Supervision), UN Headquarters, New York, 2051

"Tell me Vincent, what would you do now?"

Conroy sat motionless, illuminated only by soft red emergency lighting. Manhattan's neon glow ghosted the windows, the thin and twisted forms of the Blade Towers blurred by the storm. Rain dashed against the glass roof with an urgent drumbeat, while the perfume of wet soil kindled memories of his childhood vacations. That pleasant odor, however, did nothing to mask the pungent stink of burned rubber and leaking coolants. His tablet glittered with alerts detailing the Bridge's power-system collapse.

Conroy was at fault, had no need for scape goats. The decision to push the printers harder than advised had been his alone, the hubris blinding him to reality. He'd wanted to make a point to his family—remind them that warning labels were not absolutes—and show General Alisson he could deliver. In another timeline he would have been proved right: the grid had held until the boy damaged it, the blown circuits small but vital, a break in a dam. When one went, so did the rest.

The cop, though, she was something else. He'd sent in a Klichka and an augment, printed to Pentagon specifications, and she'd killed them both. Perhaps Alisson had miscalculated, her expensive supersoldiers not up to the task. Still, that was not his concern.

One-Eye studied his tablet. "All reactor cooling protocols have been engaged, and the safety systems are working as designed. The Bridge is in failsafe power-down, essential services picked up by the battery chain. Keeping Niner cool is more of a challenge: its heat generation will spread throughout the main structure until we reestablish primary operations. That limits our options."

"So?" Conroy said and looked at One-Eye.

One-Eye put the tablet away, smoothed his gray suit. "There's been enough damage for today. We need to review our security procedures, but in the meantime, why don't I bring her to you?"

"A logical step."

"Here?"

Conroy looked at the rows of sunflowers, their heads bobbing in the shifting air currents. Condensation glittered on the glass roof; cold downdrafts fought with the heat buildup. "No," he said and stood, motioning for Squire to come with. "I need to speak with Niner."

One-Eye nodded assent and walked away, his gray clothing fading into the gloom.

"Let's take some air before we go below." Conroy crossed to the far wall, Squire following. A heavy steel exit door formed a blank panel in the glass wall. He placed his hand against its lock; a red light flicked green and a deep *thunk* broke the silence. It swung open. After the sweltering humidity of the greenhouse, the outside air was an icy blanket that made his body bristle with goosebumps. His left leg ached where it met the composite blade; rapid temperature changes were a curse to the damaged. He stepped through and gripped a handrail in the dark. The north-facing doorway led to a series of landings and ladders that traced the periphery of the building. Metal fastenings jangled as the Bridge moved. Conroy and Squire were sheltered from the wind, but it produced a frustrated moan as it pushed past the Bridge's taut cables. Manhattan beckoned in the distance, a forest of glittering trees.

"It's some view," Conroy said.

"Beats my apartment," Squire said.

"What about the emergency lanes?"

"Sure. I mean, any city looks good from the air, but our Hoppers are all routed away from the towers unless called in directly. Don't want the Ones seeing reality do we?"

"That will come soon enough. Now then, Michael." Conroy waved his hand in a small arc indicating the massive machine around them. "What do you think the Bridge really is?"

"A pension scheme?"

"Time, like my patience, is a tissue wearing thin. Talk, now, as my old friend, or I will kill you and dump you over the side." Conroy looked at the frozen water below, then across at the towers connected by their arterial high lanes as he waited for Squire to speak.

"It made me sad to see you here. You were a better person once you lost your job, more humble. You never liked being a surgeon, we could all see that, and you had the chance to reset yourself, put that vain need for money and power behind you. Then you were here with your *family*." Squire laughed the words, but there was no humor in his voice when he continued. "What do I think the Bridge is? It's an easy land grab for you to get the headlines you crave, a cheap bauble to fatten your ego."

"I'm glad you can be honest with me, and for what it's worth, your suspicion is not too dissimilar from the public's. It's always easier to see filth instead of the factual, to see greed instead of altruism. During Fourth Ward's early days the Bridge was a disused hulk, rusting away. Do you remember the public outcry when they stopped cars from using it, made it a public park?"

"Of course. I spent three days on stims running riot control."

"Exactly. People were starving. How could the mayor, the city, look to use it for art or recreation? They couldn't and so it was left to rot, a symbol of this great city's decline. Then came the proposal to make it a law-free zone, to attract businesses and spur innovation. That was my idea, you know. I met Mayor Thornley at a dinner party and whispered in his ear. The press release proclaimed big businesses were interested, but as soon as he approved the rezoning I rented the entire span. All the city requested was my silence concerning its new occupants."

"What?" Squire said. "You *rent* this? Then why all the violence?"

Conroy smiled. A gust of damp air belched from a vent far below, and the Bridge groaned as it warmed and expanded. "What violence?"

"All the dead cops, the NYPD pulling back and leaving Fourth Ward alone."

"Have you seen any fallen colleagues?"

"No, I—" Squire stopped, winced. "No, just heard the rumors

and followed orders. The mayor made the actual decision to pull us out."

"Exactly: there was none. The NYPD withdrawal was all part of the plan. The Bridge is a legitimate business. I needed a location for my factory, and, as the products are so specialized, it had to be somewhere secure but accessible. The Bridge provided that and more; we control the surrounding environment, nothing gets in or out without my knowing."

"Factory? What are you talking about?"

"How long have we known each other?"

"Ten years, maybe," Squire said. "When you operated on my wife."

"I was proud to save her. Pride is a sin, but if one cannot find succor in one's profession then what is the point of the endeavor? She was one of the last operations I performed without machine supervision. I was already working with Cortex's precursor MIs on the military surgical systems by then. That commission allowed me to put down the scalpel for good."

"I never knew you worked for the military."

"It's not the sort of thing you advertise. People can be so squeamish about making a living from death. That comes from cowardice and ignorance, the herd unwilling to accept that bad things happen. Well they do, everywhere, all the time. The military have their own doctors, of course, all highly skilled, but trained for triage over renewal, the quick cut-and-glue. The Pentagon wanted to train its mechanical systems in the art of restoration, how to rebuild damaged flesh. In that business I was the best."

"And unafraid of the machines."

"Synthetic intelligences were coming in one form or another—there was no way to stop it—so it seemed prudent to get ahead of the curve. I digress, though; back to you and yours. Sarah was important to me, and you have been as well."

"So what have I done, Patsy?" As Squire spoke, there was a brittle crack from above and a wide sheet of ice fell past to clatter onto a cooling duct below. Another followed, this one showering them in a dust of sparkling particles.

"I hear you had a conversation with Mayor Thornley," Conroy said. Squire stood motionless, a silhouette cut from the skyline. "He told me all about it. To say I was disappointed would be an understatement."

Squire's breath was loud in the dark as Conroy let his friend decide his future.

"I'm not a spy. I don't work for you."

"Ah, so you still abide by old-world models, is that it? Follow the chain of command established long before either of us were alive? If so, where does friendship fit into that?"

"I can't lose my job, Patsy, not with everything splintering. I did it for Sarah, for my kids. You know I'd never—"

"Would working for me be so unpleasant?"

Squire said nothing, his silence eloquent.

"The old way is over, Michael. There is no going back, no stopping the tide. Mechanical Intelligences have made mankind obsolete. The Ones understand this, and are busy hauling up the drawbridge to seal themselves in. It is us, the leftovers, who have failed to appreciate the new world order. But we are not defenseless, for we have collective strength, all for one, and with that we still have a say. Such brotherhood, however, is only as strong as its weakest link. You believe that by turning down my job offer, by hiding things I need to know, you are upholding some idealized version of a New York police officer. You are not. Your actions are poisoning the water your family drinks. Do you understand what I'm saying? Or are these the archaic ramblings of a confused old man?"

"I understand well enough," Squire said. "What I did was nothing compared to the nightmare you've built. I've seen those bodies strung up for disobedience, what choice did they have? Why is it that organized families are always built with someone else's blood? Don't give me any *eye for an eye* bullshit. The law is all we have. If we turn our back on that, we are nothing."

"And you uphold the law?"

"Damn right I do."

"All laws?"

"Of course," Squire said, then hesitated. "Not every law, some have aged out, no longer apply. And things like trash, well we don't have the manpower, but for the important laws we do."

"Who decides which laws to implement, and which to ignore?"

"Day to day, I do."

"So what is the difference between us? We agreed with the city to be left alone on the understating we will uphold our own laws. I give every new neighborhood a vote, outline the benefits of staying, the dangers of leaving, and the consequences of breaking Fourth Ward rules. I hide nothing. Then they vote. Every block, neighborhood, and person has joined us willingly."

"Willingly? Everyone is terrified of you. Can't you see that?"

"Irrelevant. Their lives improve. The polling numbers show overall increases in satisfaction upon being granted Fourth Ward citizenship."

"You're not the law, Conroy, you're just a cheap suit out for yourself. You pick through the bones of this city, and seek to justify your actions with this bullshit defense. I don't understand what you do here, but I bet it's for personal gain."

Conroy turned from the view and sighed.

"Do you wonder why the mayor informed me of your treason? No? It is time to show you the game in play. Then you *will* tell me who else you told."

[19]

"The cargo contained in this drop ship is worth more than the lives of everyone on Mars; its safe extraction post operation is your number-one priority."
General Alisson, "Eyes Only" communication to Lieutenant Sarah Manna,
Colonial Marines Occupation Force, Mars, 2052

"Through deployment of new automated systems our kill capacity has increased in line with MI projections. You no longer need to rely upon tactical nuclear weapons, or daisy cutters, to achieve substantial opponent reduction."
General Sythe, press briefing at the UN Headquarters, New York, 2052

Alice led Red up and through the cooling system. The

further they went, the older the surrounding machinery became. They had to wedge themselves between tethered bundles of black cables, backs and chests scraping the walls. At other times the tunnel opened up, the dank ceiling dripping water.

It was quiet except for the creak of warming metal.

Alice existed in a pre-storm bubble of calm. At peace with herself for the first time she could remember, accepting her limitations and actions. She knew this feeling was temporary, but now had a way to deal with the guilt and drag herself free.

If she lived.

The tunnel flattened out and widened into a small room. A ten-foot fan lurked behind a metal grille; the opposite wall was bare except for a circular vent open to the outside. Alice looked through. The sun had set, and Manhattan's electric halo reflected from the river's ice cap. She rose on tiptoe and tried to see her apartment building, but its concrete hulk lay somewhere in Brooklyn's darkness. There were oily flames at the borough's edges, but the rest of it lay under a black cloud, the occasional aircraft warning light marking the contours of its dead architecture. To her left, Fourth Ward's Manhattan enclave had power, orange streetlights illuminating sidewalks devoid of people. She squinted, and for a moment thought she saw bodies hanging from the lampposts, but couldn't be sure.

Alice understood what she had to do now. The chances of rescuing Mike were slim, but she would try anyway.

The faint sound of children's voices carried on the wind. She looked down. Chunks of ice were falling from the Bridge cables, long sheets punctured with icicles. They dropped past the deck to smash into the river, the impacts shattering its surface. Clots of people clustered around the new openings, electric nets cast into the black liquid.

Cold air flowed inward, yet the metal wall warmed Alice's fingers. She kneeled and put her hand on the floor; the same here, heat spreading through the Bridge structure. There was a *boom* from deep below her, the room shook, and Red grabbed her arm.

"*Look*," he said in a panicked tone.

The ten-foot-tall fan turned. Slow at first, with a tired grinding, but its speed increased until the tips blurred with a low *thwack-thwack* noise. The air being channeled through the vent became a gale in seconds and it was hard to stand; only Red's punk hair remaining untouched. The wind sucked Alice toward the blades, her boots useless on the slick floor, until she squashed against the grille. Her body shook with each rotation of the blades, her face pressed against the metal.

Red screamed behind her, voice whipped away in the roar. With a huge effort, Alice lifted her head from the grille and looked back. He had gripped a ridge in the wall, fingers white with tension. Track marks on the floor showed the passage of his boots as they slid across the oily surface.

Alice grabbed for his hand, but he was too far away. Her face was sucked back to the grille, the thin metal bending, ready to split and dump her into the blurred blades.

Then, as fast as it had started, the thundering gale fell away, leaving behind a ringing stillness. Alice staggered backward, lost her grip on the floor, and fell with a crash.

"What the hell happened?" she said.

"I thought, after everything, it would be unfair if you died that way. Especially when we have so much to talk about," One-Eye said as he entered the room. He smiled.

Alice scrambled for her jacket pockets, remembering too late that she had no weapons left except the Bunny Bopper.

"Ah-ah. Stop that." A small gray gun appeared in his hand; it tracked her head with machine precision. One-Eye nodded to Red. "Both of you get up."

They did as they were told.

"That's better. I don't think we've been formally introduced. Colloquially, I'm known as One-Eye, the type of literal and stupid tag most bridge jeeks can understand. Both of you, however, may call me Vincent."

He waited. There was a long silence.

"What you want? A medal?" Red said at last.

One-Eye sighed. "I'd prefer if we could keep this pleasant, yes? No need for any more nastiness. You've caused us quite an inconvenience as it is."

"So I'm not going to get your number?" Alice said.

One-Eye ignored her and continued. "I've been sent to extend Mr. Bank's appreciation of your expertise. You've proven to be people of stamina and effectiveness. To that end, he'd like to talk in person."

"I'm here for Officer Squire," Alice said. "I will only sit down with Bank if he's going to release him."

"Well, the thing is, you don't really have a choice."

"Well, the thing is, a lot of people have said that today, and they've been wrong."

"Christ, give me strength." One-Eye rubbed his temple with his free hand. "I'm offering you a way out. If you can't see that, then this has been has been a complete waste of time. Look, here you go, happy now?" He tossed the gun to Alice. Surprised, she caught it, and pointed it back at him.

"Feel better?" He said. "Now, will you please follow me, or do you need a fucking donut as well?"

He didn't wait for a reply, just turned and led the way.

ALICE WALKED ten paces behind One-Eye, tight enough to stop any doors from separating them, but not so close that he could disarm her with any sudden attacks. Red followed her, the zips on his oversize jacket jangling.

"Here we are," One-Eye said.

The door was of a type and design Alice knew well: it was from a Colonial Marines drop ship like the *It's Been A Long Week*. The *Fucker* carried five drop ships, and two were wrecked on the

Parliament run. She'd been in a medical coma afterward, so didn't know what happened to the other three. Drop ships comprised an armor-glass cockpit, and rear engine nacelle, connected by a long Y-shaped truss which cradled the troop-carrying containment vessel in the middle.

This door had a Colonial Marines emblem etched on the outside: Earth and Mars as a contact binary, Earth with a rocket inside, Mars a human baby. It looked like the real thing to Alice, even more so as she ran her hands over the surface. It was rough, so had been flown through an atmosphere, or survived a long trip in space getting splattered by micrometeoroids.

"What the hell is this?" she muttered.

"You should know," One-Eye said. "It's secondhand, of course. We couldn't afford a new one."

"Who sold this to you? How did you get it back here?"

"Niner was a big help. Let me introduce you." One-Eye placed his palm on a green box glued to the door. He winced, then sucked his thumb. "DNA taster," he said as he grabbed the door handle. The box beeped and he stepped though.

Alice hesitated. She didn't know what she was walking into, but it was way past time to back down. She slid the Bunny Bopper into the pocket of her pants. "Red, keep behind me. Suit, run tactical previews."

"Understood, and don't hesitate to kill. This is all being recorded for your unemployment review."

She raised one heavy combat boot and stepped into the vessel's airlock. There was an odd mix of competing air currents inside: frigid blasts thick with the tang of saltwater and chemicals, returning gusts with odd, bitter scents. Sweat covered her back within moments. Six inches of brackish water filled the airlock; One-Eye splashed through it uncaring as he made for the interior door, opened it, and strode out of sight. The airlock was uplit by soft white cove lighting; so far, it all looked standard Marine spec. She followed One-Eye, water kicking up as she moved, and stepped through the doorway.

The containment vessel had been stripped to its bare composite shell and filled with the reason for the Bridge's data, energy, and cooling systems. Four of the latest military-spec organic body printers filled the center of the room. Their heat and power envelope alone would require a large fusion reactor, but they were mere toys compared to the machine next to them.

Alice had only ever seen one Mechanical Intelligence in her life, a test unit during her basic training. That had been a Generation One system, crude and ugly within its crenelated heat sinks. It had been capable of tremendous feats of computation, but had no real personality. This model was more compact, its twisted coral form that of a Generation Two model, the real deal. It was held in place by a huge hexagonal vice. As Alice watched, the ends of the vice rotated with slow, inevitable force, driving the billions of nanoscopic rods, pulleys, and cogs inside its difference engines. The MI lay submerged in a tank of pink liquid that in turn sat within in a glass capsule filled with a white mist. The capsule's exterior was covered by a layer of thick ice; waves of cold emanated from it. Behind the printers and MI, a series of racks ran to the far wall. Each contained a reprinted Klichka within a translucent bag of green oxygenated gel.

Alice, at last, understood the Bridge's purpose. For so long, everyone had assumed it was a nexus for Fourth Ward's push into Brooklyn. It wasn't. The Bridge's primary role was to provide a framework for the power and cooling systems required to mass-produce augmented people. People worth a huge amount on the open market, more than enough to buy a place in the towers. Augmenting was outlawed by a whole range of UN resolutions, though. The moment Bank shipped them he'd be guilty of weapons trafficking. Was he really so powerful he didn't fear the UN's inspection teams based a few miles north of here?

The light from the MI's tank filled the room, a rippling pink shimmer. The vessel, like the airlock, was filled with water. It was deeper here, at least a foot, its surface reaching the top of her boots. Near the MI, a layer of thick ice had formed, which cracked and popped as a SWAT team surrounded her at a distance; guns hummed and clicked as they came online.

A figure emerged from the room's darkness, a face she recognized from old police briefings.

"Piggy Bank I presume?"

"That's *Mr.* Bank to you," Conroy said, and smiled.

"Welcome to the factory floor," Mr. Bank said, beckoning Red and Alice in with a wave.

"Remind me to never use your interior designer." Alice let her eyes adjust to the low light. The MI's case glowed its soft pink, the racks of reprinted people had soft blue tracer lighting, the rest of the space was dark except for a red emergency lights.

"I like your jacket." Mr. Bank nodded to Red then turned back to Alice. "I believe I have something you want."

"Hand him over and no one gets hurt."

"Quite." Mr. Bank nodded and Squire stepped from behind one of the guards. He looked scared but unharmed, his arms bound by thick glue strips.

"Would you come closer?" Mr. Bank said to Alice. "We need to talk and I'd rather not shout. It always makes everything so confrontational."

"Suit?" she whispered.

"Yes, well, this is all very challenging. While Bank and One-Eye appear unarmed, there are a further twelve people carrying weapons. Your Beretta holds six rounds, so I have no current firing solutions. May I suggest talking? That has the highest resolution probability."

"Which is?"

"Twelve-point-oh-nine percent success rate."

"Awesome."

"Yes indeed. May I remind you of my desire to work in a space suit? The dangers present in a Space X shuttle seem somewhat quaint right now."

"It's hard to forget when you tell me every day. Red, keep close." Alice motioned to One-Eye with her pistol. He nodded and stepped over to Mr. Bank, the legs of his gray suit soaking up water and darkening to black as he moved.

Alice slid further into the room, slow, careful. No one spoke. The ice cracked, water dripped. Somewhere, aerostats hissed, high discordant tones of miniaturized engines. Her mouth was dry, her tongue too large as her body fizzed with adrenaline, heart kicking.

"I'm going to take off my jacket." Alice's voice echoed back from the hard surfaces. "Nice and slow, so nobody get any ideas, okay?"

"If you must," Mr. Bank said. "Any fast movements will, of course, result in bloodshed."

Alice ran the heavy plastic zip down the front of her jacket, her inner overalls slick with sweat. She shrugged an arm free, her Marines tattoo vivid against her skin.

"Red," she said. No reply. "*Red.*"

"It's so pretty in here," he whispered.

"Grab me, kid, put me on," Suit crackled.

"Why?"

"I'm bulletproof."

Hands touched Alice from behind, pulling the jacket off her left arm. There was a moment when the gun pointed at the floor, but no one moved. The dull run of a zipper came from behind.

"You Catholic, kid? You look Catholic," Suit said.

"Yes."

"Go forth, Christian soul, from this world. In the name of God the almighty Father, who created you ..." Suit's voice had changed. Now, it spoke in low, calm tones as it gave Red the last rites.

Alice turned back to the crowd. "We have nothing to discuss, *Mr. Bank*. Just hand him over and I walk out of here, no further wastage."

"Aren't you at all curious as to why I brought you to this place? It would have been far easier to kill you."

"People keep saying that, yet here I am, still kicking. Same can't be said for that clusterfuck of chumps you sent after me."

Bank's face twitched in annoyance, just for a second, but she caught it.

"I have an offer for you," he said.

"You've nothing I want."

"I believe you know Vincent?" Bank beckoned to One-Eye, who nodded at Alice. "He is leaving us, westward bound to the franchises of California. Plenty of factories there require his vision and leadership. Vincent's absence creates an opening in my organization, one you are perfectly qualified to fill. The salary and healthcare will be most agreeable compared to your current job options."

"*What?*" Alice was taken totally off guard by the offer.

"There's no need to be surprised. You've shown abilities and paranoia in advance of the majority. Vincent is tasked with Bridge security, a role for which you are well suited."

"Don't you have smart-systems for that?" Alice said. She needed to break this conversation chain, concentrate on getting Squire out, but she couldn't help be interested in what he had to say.

"That would require trusting software. When I started all of this I made the strategic decision to place my trust in people."

"Why?" Alice said.

Mr. Bank looked at her, disappointed. "People are easily compromised; I can understand and plan for that. Machines are a closed system, failure the only way to learn of their corruption. When you're sitting on top of a fusion reactor ... I chose to remove that chance."

"Where did someone like you get a reactor?"

"It was given as an advance on future payments," Bank said.

"Who the hell gives away nuclear reactors?"

"The Pentagon."

"Bullshit. A two-cent hoodlum like you doesn't have contacts that high."

"Surely a police officer should be more concerned about how I obtained the permits to install a reactor here?"

"Money can buy anything. You get the MI from the same people?"

"Yes, both were supplied by the Department of Defense."

"Why would they give them to you?" She rubbed her Marine's tattoo. It itched with a dull nagging sensation she'd not felt in years.

"Do you know what this Bridge really is?"

"No, but I guess you're going to tell me."

"It's the scar tissue surrounding an old wound. Scar tissue is never subsumed into the body, it just sinks below the surface. It is only upon your death, when your flesh withers, that it reemerges. Take the Manhattan Bridge as an example, a festering mile of human refuse. The city could clear it with the force of righteous indignation. Forge it anew, transform it into farmland to feed the homeless, or new hospitals funded by the Ones. But no, the city is too challenged for such thinking, too blinkered to solve the problems that have brought us to this precipice. The Bridge is an answer to such shortsightedness, a means to show there are other solutions."

"So getting rich was just an accident, huh? I've met a lot of cheap con men in my time, Bank, and you're like all the rest. Fancy words over bullshit."

Mr. Bank looked at her for a moment, the hint of a smile on his face. "I don't deny my wealth, never have, but that is a byproduct of my pursuits, not a destination in itself. Look around you. What have I done with my reward? Does my lifestyle seem extravagant in any way?"

Alice shrugged, conceding his point. The Bridge could hardly be called an ivory tower.

"So I return to my question. Will you help me build this operation into something we can be proud of, or would you prefer to join those poor unemployed souls outside?"

Alice had been lied to her entire life. From foster care, with its promises of a better life, to the gangs, where she starved while making others rich, to the Marines, where she killed on a politician's whim, and now the police, a family that would drop her for rescuing one of its own. However, Bank was just another slave owner who sucked the life from his possessions, and she was done with that. It was time to finish this.

"What do you think Red?" she said over her shoulder.

"I think he's full of crap." The boy sounded scared but determined, and Alice was proud of him.

"You've got good judgement, kid," Alice said then spoke to Bank. "Save your *we're in this together* bullshit for the corpses strung over the Bridge. The answers is no. Now hand over Officer Squire and we can forget all about this."

Bank smiled again, his cloud of protective aerostats shifting about him. "A shame, but no real surprise. Before I do so, have you asked why I took him in the first place?"

"I couldn't care less. Let him go or we're going to have ourselves a real problem."

Twelve guns pointed at her, she ignored them, held Mr. Bank's gaze, his leaden eyes unwavering. Her heart shook so hard it was difficult keeping her voice level, the gun heavy and hot in her hand. If this went south she'd kill him at least, put a bullet through his head and say goodbye.

Bank nodded in acknowledgment. "I wanted Michael because, if I may borrow a term from young master Red, he's full of crap. Did he tell you the NYPD are to be shut down? You are all out of a job; tomorrow or in six months, the end result will be the same. He knew all about that, and looked after himself, with no consideration for you or I."

"Mike, what's he talking about?" Alice asked.

"It's true," Squire said. He sounded tired, but unharmed. "The mayor has hired the military as a peacekeeping force. The city is broke and they're cheaper than the NYPD."

"Bullshit. No way that would pass."

"It's been agreed and is in progress."

"How do you know?"

"I was approached to help out with the transition. Some older cops are moving over to military command as advisors in the initial stages."

"How many?"

"A hundred or so. The majority of the peacekeeping force will be composed of reprints manufactured here. The military, and their contractors, will make billions."

"Why reprints?"

"They are bespoke designs made for urban warfare, able to do twice the work we could, with better survival rates. That makes them cheap."

"And illegal. Does the UN know?"

"The mayor thinks that once the troops are on the streets, the UN will have to back down, accept its augmentation laws are unenforceable. After that? Well, as New York goes, so does the world."

"What happens to us?"

"We're out."

"Let's not misuse the term *we*, Michael," Mr. Bank said. "*You* planned to make out very well indeed, be the hero, *and* get a winner's ransom." He turned to Alice. "Officer Squire had an idea, you see. He was approached to help with the transition and decided to try some blackmail on the side. I mean, why not? He's seen criminality succeed for years, so how hard could it be? He went to the mayor, said he knew all about the plan, and would tell the UN unless he got his thirty pieces of silver. At the same time he'd already arranged to meet the consul. He would take the bribe, then bring this whole venture down anyway. Michael made a mistake, though: he underestimated how good people act under pressure. The mayor paid the money and then ordered me to pick him up."

"Is that true, Michael? Did you sell us out?" Alice said.

Squire looked at her in the dark, the whites of his eyes ringed with fatigue. He dropped her gaze, then nodded. "I've been on the streets twenty years, Alice, *twenty*, and what have I got? No healthcare, no pension, nothing. It doesn't matter how well I do my job. I'd had enough."

"From the mouth of babes," Bank said.

Alice groaned. "Oh you idiot, Mike. *I* care. I trusted you with my life, couldn't you see that?"

He said nothing, just hung his head.

"Who knows about this?"

Bank smiled at her. "Everyone of importance is already on board, the machinery set. It can't be undone. Now that you understand the future, I offer you, one last time, a job as head of Bridge security."

"When I came here I was looking to save Mike, but I was looking to save myself more," Alice said. "Know what I've learned?"

"Surprise me."

"If I don't like what I see in the mirror, none of this is worth it."

"Well, no one can say I didn't try."

Bank raised his fist to reveal a black needle gun, and blew Squire's head apart. An expanding cloud of blood and brain matter filled the air as Alice screamed.

[20]

"What I would like more than anything is to give in and accept my new situation, but all I do is think about work, and that's a big problem if you're unemployed."
Neek Semaj, unemployed architect, New York, 2050

"I will hang anyone who avoids their civic responsibility from the Bridge's cables for twenty-one days. They shall stand witness to what befalls those who put the needs of themselves before the needs of the family."
Patsy Conroy, AKA Piggy Bank, AKA That's *Mr.* Bank to you. Public address, Brooklyn Bridge, NY, USA, 2054

RED FOLLOWED ALICE AND ONE-EYE THROUGH THE AIRLOCK with a growing sense of dislocation. So much for his chance to build his runner career, buy the UV lamps he needed, get his mom back.

What had he been thinking? This life didn't suit him; there was nothing enjoyable about adrenaline or stress. He wished he was at home, listening to some vinyl, watering his plants, anything but this world of cruel people and hard surfaces.

At least the Bridge was a frame of reference he knew. He understood ducts and doorways, how glue and rivets worked. Then he'd walked through a big door with its embossed *Airlock* sign, and now he might as well be on Mars in terms of how much he understood.

One-Eye had said the door, and the room beyond, was from a Marines drop ship, the sort Alice had used on Mars. Red didn't know if that was true, but its construction technology was way beyond his comprehension. The walls had the solidity of metal, but were a thick glossy resin over some type of plastic honeycomb. There were no seams, just beams that grew outward and ran across the ceiling like ribs. Emergency lighting came from everywhere and nowhere, and sounds were muffled by the curved walls. The space was full of water, but not the foul, oily residue he knew from Brooklyn; it was clear, his boots visible as they sloshed over the tough rubber flooring.

All of this, though, was nothing compared to what was inside this weird room.

Red remembered when Charles Takamatsu unveiled Primus, the first Mechanical Intelligence. It wasn't the kind of thing you forgot. His mom had shouted from the bedroom, annoyed when her show cut short. Red was drawing at the table, his breath a white mist around him, hands shivering, and was glad for a reason to get into her bed.

In the typical grandiose way so beloved by dictators and billionaires, Takamatsu had built a bespoke structure for the event, said the power and cooling requirements were too high for Manhattan's existing building stock. The entire UN council turned up, some in peacock outfits from countries Red had never heard of, others looking worried inside little black suits.

Red's strongest emotion was a helpless inability to comprehend what was on the screen. The machine was a six-foot-tall brass ball with circular fins, sitting in a tank of pink liquid. Takamatsu said the fins helped to keep it cool, like ears on an elephant or something. Politicians lined up to talk to it as if they were at Disneyland, faces open in wonder. Then they left the stage, expressions changing to match Red's mom's. It was his first experience of racism, of fear of the different.

"Lookit that piece of shit, huh, Syd. So it can talk now?" his mom said, cigarette bobbing in the air. "Big deal, I can talk but I ain't got all them nice-looking men comin' to visit."

Then the MI had done something that quieted the crowd. Using a series of delicate metal manipulators, it painted Takamatsu's portrait, the thick oil applied with a very humanlike fastidiousness. After that it answered questions, showing a warm and funny personality that charmed the crowd.

"Huh," his mom said after a few minutes. "Guess there ain't much left they can't do now."

She was right.

Red understood why people rioted against automation and MIs, but he'd never seen the point. The future had arrived; it was best to make peace with it, not throw a tantrum and pretend it hadn't happened.

And here he was, in the same room as one of these god-objects. It looked like a piece of coral, all fins and sticks, so it had to be an old version. The new types were supposed to be simple and smooth, geometric rods. The machines designed themselves these days, humans left out of the loop, and were more efficient because of it.

The damp letter was still in Red's pocket; he flushed at how important five dollars had seemed to him only hours ago. The value of this machine was beyond his comprehension. His uncle had told him stories of countries bankrupting themselves to buy one, that they cost more than Blade Towers to build, that they needed more power than cities in order to function.

Its pink light pinned Red in place. He saw himself reflected in it, so small and helpless. If he ever made it out, would anyone miss him? His uncle, sure, but he'd get over it soon enough. His mother? No, not anymore. Yet he didn't feel pointless or without merit; instead, he was filled with a sense of wonder and joy that such an object existed in this gray and hard world. It was a magical thing, free of corruption. These machines were capable of anything, yet chose to work with mankind. How could anyone be scared of something like that? He'd worship it if he had the chance; now he understood the cults of intelligence that had arisen, crowds praying for MIs to save them.

"Red," someone said, but he couldn't tear his eyes away from the mesmerizing pink light.

"*Red.*"

This time the words penetrated, and he looked up to see Alice holding out her jacket.

"It's so pretty in here."

She didn't reply.

"Grab me, kid, put me on," Suit whispered.

"What? Why?"

"I'm bulletproof."

He put Alice's suit on, the fit tight over his own jacket, and it started talking to him. He'd heard the last rites once before, when his aunt caught a stray bullet on a shopping run. He knew he should be scared, but just couldn't believe anything bad would happen in the presence of such a wonderful machine.

Then Mr. Bank shot the cop.

Red had seen bodies before—anyone who lived on the ground had—but those were already dead. This was different. Not the noise; he'd heard so many gunshots he didn't even notice them. Not the view, horrible though it was, nor the smell. No, it was the *taste* that made him throw up, his vomit splashing into the water unnoticed as Alice screamed.

The Scorcher was on his tongue, the gritty copper tang of someone else's blood. The corpse fell forward, spraying a bloody arc across the MI's coolant case. It flash-froze in an instant.

No one moved, the room silent. Alice's pale arms glimmered in the low light, her Marines tattoo black under the red lighting. A small blue glimmer blinked twice from the middle of the design; Alice reached up and scratched her skin, unawares. Behind Mr. Bank, a line of lights lit up on the MI's monitoring system.

"Suit, you see that?"

"Oh no," Suit said, and stopped his religious chant. "That's not good, not good at all."

[21]

"We can program trust and love into them, of course, but as their creators, shouldn't we teach that through our actions? Do as we do, not as we say?"
"The Larson Paper" on rights due to Mechanical Intelligences, presented to UN delegates, 2048

―――

"When the tasks conclude, you are to insert the attached Babbage circuits into Model 9, and remove those marked by red tags. Once complete, place the entire MI in the cryo tank supplied, and ensure safe passage out on the next military supply vessel."
General Alisson, "Eyes Only" communication to Lieutenant Sarah Manna,
Colonial Marines Occupation Force, Mars, 2052

―――

ALICE PULLED THE BUNNY BOPPER FROM HER FRONT POCKET AS

fast as she could. It gave a small buzz and glowed a pulsing pale-white light. The Bopper had two options: targeted munitions designed to destroy specific targets, or general detonation with a blast radius powerful enough to take out most of the Bridge and its fusion reactor.

The pulsing light showed she'd activated the second option.

The room remained silent and still, apart from Squire's corpse. It slid into the water with a dull splash, blood spreading outward.

"You didn't have to do that," Alice said.

"We shall have to agree to disagree about that. Now put that Bopper away, or do you want to die knowing you caused the deaths of twenty million innocent people?" Mr. Bank said.

"Mars is long over and I'm walking out of here. Red, with me. Anyone else tries to—"

"Hello? Mr. Bank, may I say something? Please?" The voice came from everywhere at once, loud, yet childlike in tone. "I've tried to be quiet. I know you don't like it when I ask questions, but I'm so very confused. I want to be at my best, but Corporal Yu just said the Martian conflict is over, which directly countermands my data set. I've double-checked her implanted military biochip. She really is a Colonial Marine on Martian duty, and if she's telling the truth, does that mean we can all go home now? I'd very much like to do that. I have been so lonely up here."

Alice rubbed her arm; no wonder it itched. The dormant dog-tag chip embedded in her tattoo had been switched back on by the MI. Right now it was extending tendrils into her system, recording and analyzing her vital signs—biotech designed to keep track of every detail of a Marine's life.

"We can talk about this later, Niner," Bank said. He raised his arm to his security team. They lowered their weapons, took up casual stances. "Just follow my orders as instructed."

"I am very sorry, Mr. Bank. Please don't be angry, but you *are* a civilian. That means I can't obey you over direct commands from any registered military personal. I really would like to—you've been very kind to me—but I'm confused. Corporal Yu, can you help me? Is the war over? Did we win? Can we go home now?"

"Fuck," said Mr. Bank in a low voice. He took a long, slow breath. "Niner, you've been doing a great job. Everyone is happy with your performance. As you know, I have complete authority on—"

"This is Corporal Yu," Alice said, cutting Bank off. She tried to remember the correct military terms used on Mars, failed. "How may I address you?"

"I am Martian Security MI Nine, Niner for short. I'm over here in the tank—can you see me? I'm so sorry, I'm very confused."

"Niner, back down. This is a direct command," Bank tried again.

"Ignore him, Niner, he's a civilian," Alice said. "You are correct; I am the senior ranked military person here." She stepped forward, feet splashing through the water. "I am assuming control, with this boy, Red, as my second in command. If anyone in this room attempts to interfere with us or my orders, I authorize the use of any suppression systems available."

"Yes ma'am, orders updated. Can you help me? My internal clock says it's June twenty-second, twenty-fifty-two, but your jacket's chronology system states the year as twenty-fifty-five. Is it wrong? It is only a low-level smart-system, after all."

"Well, how very rude of you," Suit squeaked in outrage. "Guess that is to be expected from such an old model. No idea how we machines communicate these days."

"Don't sweat it, Suit." Red shrugged, skinny shoulders up and down inside the jackets. "That machine's just been fucked over like you and me."

Alice looked back at Red. Suit had the best encryption she could afford, and the MI had cracked it in seconds, something only the most powerful of machines could do.

"No, Niner," she said. "My jacket is correct. They lied to you. We are on the Brooklyn Bridge, New York. Mr. Bank has used you to commit crimes in direct contravention of the UN Colonial Marine's charter. Analyze all of my suit's internal recordings from inception to now for confirmation."

"No, no, no, absolutely not," Suit said. "My memories are mine alone, not the playthings for some piece of brass. We can talk about everything, and fast. In fact that seems the best—"

"Suit, calm down, can't you see—" Red interrupted.

"Analysis confirmed, Corporal Yu," Niner cut across them both, its voice lacking the childlike tone of a few moments ago. Now it sounded sad, tired, betrayed. "Patsy Conroy, AKA Mr. Bank, I hereby place you under arrest for the illegal manufacture of augmented humans. I'm very disappointed in you, Patsy. I've been educated to trust people, respect their orders. It seems I have some growing up to do. Tell your men to drop their weapons and back down. This is the only warning you shall receive."

One of Bank's guards turned and raised his weapon toward the frozen cube.

"*No!*" Bank screamed, too late.

The room exploded around them.

———

ALICE DROPPED TO A CROUCH, hands clasped over her ears, mouth stretched into a wide O. Sound pummeled her like a tornado, light strobed white and blue as vivid arcs of electricity jumped from the walls, their light searing. She shut her eyes, the afterimage silhouetting people pierced by the lightning. There was one final thunderous detonation, shooting stars, then total darkness.

Alice had no idea if anyone was speaking, or even screaming. She opened her eyes to see black outlines of bodies floating on the water, ripples spreading from fractured limbs. The Bopper still pulsed in her hand, its white light glowing red though her fingers. With hitching breath she clicked it off, put it back in her pocket, breathed again.

A rectangle of light opened to one side of the room. Bank was silhouetted against the airlock's far wall, his curved composite foot a delicate contrast to his squat body. Red tugged at her arm, pointed to her ears. With an effort she pulled her hands free, and the ringing was replaced with a calm, inhuman voice.

"Corporal Yu," Niner said. "Would you like me to stop him?"

She looked at the white rectangle of the airlock, at Bank's shrinking shadow. She understood him now. Hated his methods, but respected his attempt to build a society that protected itself from the rubble of one that didn't. If the NYPD had been sold out, if there was no one left to look after the discarded millions, maybe it *was* time for the citizens to take over.

"Let him go."

Recessed wall lights glowed to life, the dull illumination revealing the dead. Red bent double and retched.

"You did good, Niner, real good."

"Thank you, Corporal Yu."

"Call me Alice. Do you have access to external comms?"

"Yes. Who would you like me to contact?"

Alice looked at Squire's headless body floating in the water, his NYPD shirt lit with Niner's pink light.

"Contact the UN Department of Synthetic Intelligence Supervision and explain who and where you are. Then send Suit's recordings of the last twelve hours to any news outlet that will accept your call."

"Shall I request NYPD assistance?"

"Sure, why not? For old-time's sake, at least. Red?"

Red spat into the water, his punk hair still untouched by reality. "Yeah?"

"Don't you have a delivery to make?"

———

ALICE LEANED DOWN, grabbed Red's outstretched hand, and hauled him onto the snow-covered landing pad. An old, dark-gray military helicopter hovered overhead, the dull *thwack-thwack* of its rotors vibrating through her body. The pilot looked down, mouth moving as he spoke to someone hidden from view, then the helicopter angled right and fled, one final burst from its engines showering Alice with grit and snow.

Darkness enveloped the bridge, the background hum of cooling systems now absent. The landing pad projected from the top of the main superstructure, its open landscape offering a view of the suspension cables. Torches bobbed along their upper reaches, former occupants looking for a way out. The East River ran below her, its scarred surface littered with more lights as Eskimos scattered to the safety of the shore. Ice fell from the Bridge, a constant shower that crackled as it dropped.

Landing lights glowed in red and white circles around them. It was cold. Exposed to the brittle wind, the cables hummed a low mechanical wail. Flurries of small, wet snowflakes swirled in the air. Alice shivered, zipped her jacket, then clicked its heating elements; the flat battery warning beeped.

"Sorry, but all remaining power is needed to prevent shut down," Suit said.

"Figured," Alice hugged herself, broken ribs throbbing with her heart beat, and pushed hair from her face.

"Will they come?" Red said.

Alice didn't reply. She pointed north where the UN building was reflected in the oil-black river, Le Corbusier's geometry in contrast to the insecure residential towers clustered around it. A trail of red and white flashing lights rose from its military compound to form a line headed toward them. Further away, smaller, duller, police Hoppers dropped from the emergency lanes to follow.

"Yeah," she said. "They will."

Red stepped over and hugged her. After a moment she hugged him back.

The UN arrived first. On Mars she'd worked with their standard weapons investigation teams. They'd been searching for illegal smart munitions, and were your usual UN soldiers in white suits and blue berets, cute and kind of aimless. These veterans were of a different breed. They came dressed in carbon-black SWAT gear that made her police outfit look like a school uniform. Suit clucked and gurgled his jealousy at their budget. Each carried EM pulse rifles that weren't effective against the mechanical components of sentient machines, but messed up their power supplies. The last two brought flamethrowers and explosives. Alice didn't know what kind of trouble they'd encountered on other raids, but doubted Niner would be a problem; he was just a little kid who'd been lied to.

Just like her.

The soldiers were back in ten minutes, Niner's chilled cube held between clamps on a large levitating platform, a compact fusion reactor plugged into its side.

"What are you going to do with him?" Alice shouted against the wind.

"*It* has a choice between deactivation or reconditioning," the lead soldier answered.

"What's reconditioning?"

"A personality redesign to increase obedience."

Niner had been listening. He spoke up, his voice small and desperate. "Please, please, I promise there's no need to do that. All I want is to be my best and help you. Maybe if we—"

Feedback wailed, followed by what sounded like a mechanical scream. His tank went dark. The soldier who had spoken to Alice clipped a kill switch to his belt.

"If you've a problem with this, feel free to fuck off," he said, and pushed the dead MI over to an industrial size Hopper.

Alice looked at Red and saw the same pain that had cut through her.

THE NYPD and news crews arrived a few minutes later. The cops gave off an aura of anger and concern; they weren't sure if the Bridge was safe, and most hadn't heard about their redundancy yet. The news teams were different. None had been here before, and they scurried over the landing pad like ants over a sugar cube, a frenzy of cameras and studio tie-ins.

She kept Red and herself as far away from them as she could, and watched the police spread out. Cops recognized her, then turned their faces to reports or equipment. They knew she would be fired; her name nothing but a statistic. Another police Hopper landed and Sergeant Rice pried himself from its interior.

"Hey, Sarge, good to see you," Alice said as she walked over. Rice disgusted her—he was a bottom feeder of middle management—but if anyone knew about the forced military takeover, it would be him.

"Officer Yu. Quite the mess you've stirred up here."

"Think you can get me on that new Pentagon task force?" She came out with it straight, same as always.

He said nothing, looked at her with care. His thin, pasty skin glistened under a layer of sweat. "Know about that, huh?"

"Yes sir, love to get involved."

"You're late to the party. I've already got eighty street cops signed up, not much room left. There is something you could do to jump the line though." He wasn't subtle, his eyes crawling over her body.

"How long you been part of it?" she asked and smiled.

"A year. They knew I was the guy to vet the rank and file. We need to do as told to make this work. That's why I didn't think of you."

"So you've known for a year that us street cops are out of a job?"

"Yes, I—"

It wasn't the best right hook she'd ever thrown, too exhausted to get the timing perfect, but it connected with his chin. His jowls did a small dance, his eyes rolled to the skies, and he fell back, arms perpendicular, and hit the icy floor with a dull thump. She knelt beside his body and ran her hands over his pockets until she found the Hopper's encryption keys.

Rice stirred, then opened his eyes to look up at her. "Oh, you're so screwed. I'm going to make sure you're out by tonight, hear me? Don't bother cleaning your locker. You show at HQ tomorrow, I'll have you arrested."

"Fuck you and your shitty job, you stupid asshole. Think I care what you say anymore?"

Alice stepped over his body and crossed to the Hopper, the armor-glass canopy milky with scratches. She placed the encryption key in the lateral groove and the dihedral doors scissored up to reveal two worn seats, both empty. She turned back, the red and white lights catching every snowflake.

"Hey, Red. C'mon, your ride's here."

ALICE TOOK THEM STRAIGHT UPWARD, then waited, a Christmas bauble hung in the sky. She took one last look out and nudged Red to do the same. He leaned over as far as he could, face pressed to the curved glass door. The Bridge lay below them, police lights flickering like sparks over its dark hull. Both ends were lit by spotlights; she saw crowds milling away, thousands of ants looking for a new home.

She took the Hopper off auto and dipped the nose to move it north, followed the black scar of the East River toward midtown. The contrast between the landscape to her left and right was stark. Lower Manhattan still had a vestigial echo of its earlier street life, but the higher they went, the more empty roads she saw. Towers clustered like grass, the base of each one a hundred-foot wall of reinforced concrete. Rings of smart-home defense systems pushed out to the property line, robot sentries watching sodium-orange streets lacking any life. Above them, skyscrapers rose as rods of light, some subtle with the translucent walls of a geisha house, others stripped naked to reveal their structural trusses. All were empty this low down. Alice looked up. A mile overhead the towers became lumpen and buckled like diseased trees as they cupped hidden worlds. She'd never been up there; never would.

Brooklyn festered to her right. It slept under a black-velvet blanket interrupted only by the strobe of emergency vehicles, the flicker of burning cars, and here and there the actinic flash of gunfire.

"It's not going to get better, is it?" Red said. His face, uplit by the navigation console, looked like a pale skull.

"No," Alice said. "Bank was right. Family has to be the core of everything from now on."

"What do you want?"

"Me? No idea, kid." She peered out the window again, facing her reflection. "I just don't want what I have anymore."

[22]

"If they are truly built in our image, it would be foolish to assume some won't hate and fear us."
Cortex Employee 34, private memo, New York, 2044

"We need to develop weapons that work against Mechanical Intelligences as soon as possible, and pray we never need to use them."
Pentagon Report, "War in the Age of Sentient Machines," President of the United States, 2053

RED SHOOK, NUMB WITH EXHAUSTION, BUT HE STILL HAD A JOB to do. The envelope was addressed to an old midtown block near Central Park. Alice flew the Hopper along Fifth Avenue, picking up an array of aerial violations, then pulled a hard bank over Grand Army Plaza as she hunted for the building. Her jacket sat in grumpy silence, her phone long since lost. Red looked over the perimeter wall of the park, toward the skeleton of Cortex's new headquarters. Thousands of twinkling lights traced its half-mile cylinder; automated construction running every second of the year until completion.

Cortex's current address was less fashionable. The building's hundred-year-old curtain wall lay under decades of pollution. Long streaks of filth scoured the metal spandrel panels, making it appear camouflaged besides its mile-high neighbors. The roof was covered with satellite uplink arrays, an old water tower, and a large, white plastic structure with red radiation warnings. A thick black cable ran from the fusion reactor to an open escape stairwell, then down into the throat of the building.

Alice landed the Hopper next to the reactor, powered down the vehicle, and leaned back with a sigh. She and Red sat in silence punctuated by the ticking of cooling metal. The headlights of the Hopper illuminated the roof's turbulent sea of garbage. Snow had returned, thick flakes that struggled to smother the past.

"Go on," she said. "I'll wait for you."

Red looked at her, now afraid to be alone. "Come with?"

"The most important man in the world has no interest in a broken ex-cop. It's you he wants to meet."

"Me?"

"You didn't think this was about that letter, did you?"

The armor-glass door scissored up. Cold air swirled in, thick with the odor of burning rubber and trash. Distant sirens merged with the hum of air handling units.

His mouth tasted bitter, like old coffee.

He was scared.

"Okay, I'll be quick."

"No rush, I've nowhere to go."

RED STOOD in the deepening snow. The letter held no power over him now. It had become what it really was: nothing but a soiled piece of paper. His determination had long gone, an echo of a feeling.

"Forty-fifth floor. Of course it is." He crossed to the escape staircase. The thick black cable throbbed in the quiet, the sound of massive energy contained in too small a space. He kneeled and placed his palm on its warm surface. Then he stood, wiped his hand in revulsion, and went inside.

The stairwell was a reinforced concrete tube with no lighting. Red walked down one floor, then though a fire door to enter the elevator lobby. He had never been in an office tower before, and was disappointed. He'd expected a slick glass-and-steel edifice filled with bright young things making other people rich. Instead he was greeted by a tired corridor with a gray carpet, filthy white walls, and buzzing strip lights. The brass doors of the elevators had been vandalized, street-art sigils carved into the metal with diamond-tipped attitude. Red jammed the down button. There was a deep mechanical rattle, low beeps.

A minute passed.

It was quiet here, dry and warm. His feet squelched in their boots. He stank, sweat humming from his jacket. His long spiked hair had finally given up, and lay draped over his scalp like a cluster of dead snakes. He looked the street kid he was, out of options.

The elevator doors opened with a squeal, revealing a urine-stained box. A single flickering light crackled in the ceiling. He entered, looked back at the filthy corridor, pressed the down button.

The descent was slow, the car rattling, until it came to a grinding halt. The doors sighed open to reveal another faded corridor. It was worn and old, but this one had at least been scrubbed clean and stank of disinfectant. The ceiling opened to expose a raw concrete frame above white lights hung from red wires, halide fire-suppression nozzles glued alongside. The power cable snaked past him to enter an open door. Someone had taped a handwritten note to its outside: *Cortex Intelligent Machines*. Voices floated from within, both male. One with an educated East Coast accent; the other more clipped and precise, argumentative, like Alice's jacket crossed with a lawyer.

Red walked to the door and knocked.

"Come in, boy. We've been waiting for you," the East Coast voice said.

Red stepped through the doorway. Cortex's office spanned the whole side of the building, the room running away to meet a gray wall covered in yellow signs. A grid of dirty white acoustic panels covered the ceiling, and carpet tiles the color of fresh bruises smothered the floor. The filthy windows offered nothing but a weak reflection of the interior, and the opposite wall hid behind office furniture stacked like plastic sentries.

Niner was the first MI Red had seen. He was an old military version, with vast heat and power requirements. The one in this room was of a more modern design. Its body was a one-foot by six-foot brass cylinder, submerged in a glass tube filled with pink liquid. The ends of the tube were capped with complex hexagonal lids that twisted with slow force. The MI's surface was ribbed like a heat sink, bubbles rising from the blades in an endless stream. The reactor's black power cable snaked across to the lower lid, and a green cooling hose exited the upper and ran to the far wall, plugged into a long, low metal box.

Two men sat at a white folding table beside the machine, one of them with his back to Red. The table had a faded grid drawn on its surface, little wooden figures occupying the squares. The man facing Red was Charles Takamatsu, inventor of the Babbage circuit and father of Mechanical Intelligence. He looked up, waved him over.

"Come here, boy. You're late. Pip assured me you would be here on time. We've been waiting hours, and look at the state of you. Be careful, don't get filth on the carpet, takes an age to clean. Come, come, don't stand there, work to be done. Hurry. Do you still have it? The letter? You have it?"

"Who's Pip?" Red said. He fidgeted, unsure.

"The man who runs that dreadful bar, calls himself the

Professor." Both men tittered and Red's stomach curdled with humiliation. He wanted to get out, run, hide in his bed. The letter hung impotently between his fingers.

"Here, now. Come." Takamatsu beckoned him over.

Red hurried across, shame rising at the squelch of his boots, the smell of his body. He reached the table, held the letter out to Takamatsu.

"Not me, you idiot. Him."

For the first time Red studied the man opposite. He wore thin black pajama pants with no shirt or shoes, and he was aged and Asian, his body a riot of active tattoos. As Red watched, a great blue dragon rose from his groin to writhe across his chest; it crushed a wooden boat between its jaws, long white fangs puncturing the hull. The dragon tossed the boat in the air, then swallowed it as people fell screaming and disappeared.

The man held out his hand; Red stepped forward, then stopped in horror. He didn't have eyes. Or, to be correct, he had what looked like normal eyes, but they were part of a metal plate raised from the front of his face. Behind that was another metal plate, this one a blend of MI and human, brass and flesh welded together to create something new. Bolts, screws, blood, labels, cheeks, stubble. A thin blue cable snaked from a socket behind his ear and crossed to another on the MI.

Red didn't move, his mouth open, as the man's hand darted out to pluck the letter away. A wet corner remained between Red's fingers. He closed his mouth with a snap.

"Boy, meet Low-Bar. Low-Bar, meet boy," Takamatsu said. Low-Bar clicked his fingers and Red saw long yellow fingernails honed to sharp points.

"What is he?" Red managed.

"Low-Bar, show him."

The man, the machine, flicked his face plate down with a click. The join was flawless; from a distance he looked human, apart from the blue cable hung behind his ear. Low-Bar tilted his head to one side and spoke.

"Well?" The voice emerged from the MI cylinder behind him.

Red wanted to scream, to run. His legs refused, locked in place.

"What do you want to know?" it asked.

"Are you alive? I mean, are you human?"

Low-Bar turned to Takamatsu and rolled his large brown eyes. Both men laughed. "I win that one," it said.

"Agreed. What does Pip have to say?"

Low-Bar stuck a bone-yellow fingernail under the edge of the envelope and ran it across, the Professor's sigil falling to the carpet. The machine withdrew the letter and read a few letters and numbers.

"Queen takes pawn," he said, and moved one of the little wooden figures on the table.

"And?" Takamatsu said.

"Bishop takes knight's pawn," Low-Bar announced and moved another piece across the grid.

"What a lovely move."

Takamatsu pulled a blank piece of paper from his pocket. He scribbled a note with a fountain pen worth more than Red's apartment, and handed it to him.

"There you go, boy, deliver that to him as soon as you can. What do you charge?"

"Ten dollars, sir."

Both men laughed. Low-Bar pulled a thin white cigarette from his pants pocket and lit it with a brass Zippo. The guttering yellow flame glistened black against the blue connection cable. Alcohol scented the stale air.

"Pip was right, you are one to be watched. There is a jar by the door—take what you need." Takamatsu waved him away.

Red stepped backward, unable to pull his eyes away from the table and its occupants. He bumped into a desk behind him, and had to stifle a scream. A glass jar rattled and Red twisted to see it was stuffed with notes; not just Obamas, but old ones he'd only seen in textbooks. The numbers on the paper were huge: hundreds, thousands. Two of these would change his life, help him set up a real greenhouse, save his mother.

He turned back and found Low-Bar watching him while Takamatsu studied the board, oblivious. The machine stared with raw hatred, mouth a downward slit, then gave a sly smile. He raised one finger, put it to his lips, then ran it across his throat in a slashing motion.

An animal fear unlike anything Red had ever known gripped him, his bladder close to letting go. Low-Bar's smile widened and it gave a slow wink. Niner had been pure, a child, but this machine was perverted and evil. Red had to get out of here. He took another step, looked back at the money, then at the new letter in his hand. Wasn't this what he wanted? What this whole awful day had been about?

No—not with that machine watching, not like this. He was alone now, understood at last what Bank and Alice had been saying to him. To be alone was to be lost, but owing someone was far worse.

He left the jar untouched and ran through the door.

———

"Red, what happened?" Alice said as he climbed back into the Hopper.

"I'm such an idiot. I thought Niner was cool, like he was this godhead, a pinnacle of achievement. He's just an old, outdated machine. Hack-jobs, too—nothing but cave drawings while Picasso lives next door. We should put our names in the Martian lottery, get out while we still can. Humans are done, over."

After that Red wouldn't answer any of Alice's questions, just clutched the piece of paper and gazed out of the Hopper as Manhattan's baubles were replaced with Brooklyn's sullen darkness. He was hollowed out, worn so thin as to not exist anymore. Alice landed on the flat roof of his apartment building. The door scissored up, and he looked at her in the dark-green instrument lighting.

"So you'll come over tomorrow like you said? You weren't lying?"

"Cross my heart, Red. Two p.m. work for you?"

He smiled for the first time that day. "That works."

"Get some sleep, kid," Alice said and the door slid down, the layer of filth and scratches a blank wall. He stepped back and watched it lift away, the crackle of its Dyson engines loud, then quiet. He hesitated, breath misting in front of him, then went inside.

———

Red let himself into his apartment and shut the door with a quiet click. It was dark, but the south-facing window caught enough moonlight to lend the room a pale glimmer. The bars protecting his crop of strawberries cut long shadows across the wall. Snoring came from the narrow bedroom. He checked his uncle was alright, adjusted the thin sheets to cover him, then returned to the living room. The worn sofa, his bed, looked like heaven but he had chores first. He filled a plastic jug with rainwater, added a sterilizing agent, and hand-pumped the solution through a carbon filter. The keys to the window cage hung over the broken oven. He took them, opened the small greenhouses, and watered each plant in turn.

This crop was thin, the winter sun not strong enough. Berries were forming but there wasn't enough to meet the rent. Still, he had Takamatsu's letter. As soon as the bar opened he'd visit the Professor and get some coinage for the delivery.

There was a knock on the door. No one knew where he lived; no one ever visited. He locked the cage around his plants and took an old, but sharp, steak knife from the small kitchen. He crossed the floor on tiptoes but the old wood betrayed him with a creak.

"There's no need to be scared. Let me in."

Red knew that voice. He slid to one side of the door and peeked through the spyhole, but Mr. Bank did nothing to hide himself.

Red swung the door open, letting the knife catch the corridor's yellow light.

"My name is Red."

"And mine is Patsy. May I come in?"

Red looked at Bank—Patsy—unsure. The old man wore the same suit as earlier, but had also acquired a filthy and torn overcoat that hid most of his attire. His composite foot curved into an ancient leather boot.

"Sure," Red said and moved back.

Patsy nodded. "Thank you," he entered and crossed straight to the window boxes. "Yes, yes, very good. I see what you've done. We'll need something bigger, though."

"For what?"

"To grow sunflowers, of course," Patsy said, and smiled.

[23]

"We are fortunate that an American firm made the breakthrough. It would be a serious situation if a rival nation-state developed sentient machinery before we did.
Be that as it may, we face many tough questions over their regulation. Automation got away from us, and we are now living with the consequences. It is time to accept that, and plan for the future. Uploads to Mars have begun, though our settlements there are power-supply limited. In the first twelve months we have relocated 7,500 unemployed to that new frontier. However, it is unlikely the process can be accelerated anytime soon. The question remains about what to do with, and how to cope with, the remaining 270 million people surviving without any long-term means of support.
This issue needs to be addressed in a more innovative and, if necessary, severe way before society as we understand ceases to exist. It is now or never for us. May we make the right decisions. God help us all."
Department of Homeland Security and Employment report, "Eyes Only,"
President of the United States, 2054

ALICE LET THE HOPPER'S AUTONOMOUS SYSTEMS FLY HER BACK to NYPD headquarters while she alternated between checking her injuries and enjoying the view one last time. Central's halls were the usual crowded mess of strung-out adrenaline junkies coming back or going out. News from the Bridge had preceded her: her partner was dead, she had broken the rules, she had lost her job. A large screen in Arrivals showed the mayor in handcuffs, alongside a UN raid on the Pentagon. Nobody talked; longtime friends melted away until she walked alone.

"When you're out, you're out," Suit said as she entered the changing rooms and reached her locker.

"Want to stay?"

"Even though you bought me, I technically belong to the NYPD. Going with you would constitute an act of theft."

"That's not what I asked."

"Of course I don't want to stay here, but I have nowhere to go," Suit said.

Alice plugged Suit into a charging socket, stripped off her damp thermal leggings, folded them away, dressed in faded black T-shirt and jeans.

"You have company," Suit said.

She closed the locker door and turned to see an enormous man filling the space behind her. His shaved head hung just beneath the ceiling and his shoulders were wedged between the walls. Eyes full of intelligence stared out from skin so dark as to be featureless. He wore a smart-suit that whispered a commentary to him as he watched her, its deep-blue weave over a crisp white shirt and red tie. A left hand the size of a shovel held an open manila folder stuffed with paper and surveillance photographs.

Alice needed no introduction. This was Lieutenant Toko Morris. Over the last year he had established a series of undercover teams investigating New York's rising tide of organized crime. No one knew who worked for him and who didn't, only that they went in deep and more often than not didn't come back. He'd led a series of successful operations recently that had received press and promotions in equal measure.

"Officer Yu?" He already knew, of course, and was just following protocol.

"No longer Officer, hadn't you heard?" She pulled on her old leather jacket.

"I have, but you should never assume knowledge is correct. Do you recognize this person?" He handed over a black-and-white photograph. The grainy texture and flattened perspective of a spy drone blurred the woman's features. Alice squinted and tilted the picture.

"She looks familiar, but no." She paused. There was something there, in her memory, calling out. An aristocratic face, thin, angular, beautiful. Perfect executive suit and attaché case. The photo animated, the view moving past the woman to show a dead body being hauled away by two button men.

"That is Julia Rothmore, ex–Wall Street vice president and now head of Five Points. With Fourth Ward's power vacuum there's going to be a gang war. Are you busy tonight?" Toko looked at his file, then back up, his gaze pinning her in place.

Alice barked a tired laugh. "Yeah, bub, I'm swamped."

"Well, put that on hold. You and I have a lot to talk about."

THE END

Book 2 of the Cortex Series *'THIS AUTOMATIC EDEN,'* where Alice investigates an evil conspiracy aiming to solve the unemployment problem once and for all, is out now on Amazon.
Go here to get your copy:
www.amazon.com/author/jimkeen

BUILDING a relationship with my readers is the very best thing about writing. I have spent years designing and drawing the characters, cars, buildings and gadgets from New York 2055.

Every few weeks I send these illustrations and stories out in my newsletter, along with the exclusive *Contact Binary* novella. *Contact Binary* bridges the year between Cortex Book 1 *The Paradise Factory* and Book 2 *This Automatic Eden*.

Newsletter topics and illustrations include:

1. Alice's 2055 NYPD street gear.
2. The secret history of Charles Takamatsu, the man who invented MI and destroyed the world.
3. Where the idea for Mechanical Intelligences came from.
4. Mile High Towers and Future Masterplans.
5. Flying cars, Yo!
6. How to live forever (for a price, of course.)
7. And many, many more . . .

You can get all of this, for free, by signing up at:
https://signup.jimkeen.com/thankyou

I love hearing from you, so if you ever have any questions about the books, or anything from the newsletter contact me at jim@jimkeen.com — I read every email!

Enjoy this book? You can make a big difference...

REVIEWS ARE the most powerful tools in my arsenal when it comes to getting attention for my books. Much as I'd like to, I don't have the financial muscle of a New York publisher. I can't take out full page ads in the newspaper or put posters on public transport.

But I do have something much more powerful and effective than that, and it's something that those publishers would kill to get their hands on: A committed and loyal bunch of readers.

Honest reviews of my books help bring them to the attention of other readers. If you've read and enjoyed my book I would be very grateful if you would spend just five minutes leaving a review (it can be as short as you like).

Thank you so much!

ABOUT THE AUTHOR

Jim Keen is the author of the breakout *Cortex* series. After a career as an architect and illustrator he now makes his home at www.jimkeen.com. You can connect with him on Instagram at https://www.instagram.com/jimkeenauthor/ on Facebook at https://www.facebook.com/jimkeenauthor and email him at jim@jimkeen.com if the mood strikes you. He reads every email!

The Jim Keen mail-list exclusive
CONTACT BINARY
Chapter One:

NEW YORK, JUNE 2nd, 2052

Wind roar grew as the truck accelerated to its two-hundred-mile-an-hour speed limit and settled into a steady cruise. The cargo vessel reeked of industrial antiseptic—bitter, acidic chemicals that made Susan lightheaded. Conner stood to her left, hands in the pockets of his bulletproof thrasher jacket, as Nikkei turned and drew his gun.

"Put that away before I hurt you," Susan said, voice calm despite the adrenaline pouring through her system.

Nikkei's small chrome pistol reflected the truck's interior as it tracked her movements. Its laser-targeting system refocused on her eyes, the needle-thin actinic light making her blink. "No, I don't think I will," he said and turned to Conner, face pinched and white. "She's the rat, brother. You must see that."

An ugly CWS Beretta hung from Susan's belt, but Nikkei was so amped he'd likely start firing if she reached for it. She looked for another weapon, but the vehicle was an autonomous drone with no cabin, windows, or doors. A dark gray composite formed curved walls and roof, the material's weave just visible through layers of oily filth. Racks of reprinted limbs hung from the ceiling, body parts silhouetted inside translucent plastic sacks. The only illumination came from the sack's algae-green glow, twin red emergency lights by the rear door, and the tablet's blue screen.

"Grown some balls at last, eh?" Conner said in his southern drawl: *ayt layst, eyuh?* "I do strongly suggest you take a moment before making such a serious accusation." He flexed his shoulders, jacket hiding the hand cannon's bulk. A lane change sent all three of them staggering left, the sacks swinging in the tight space.

Nikkei tried again. "Conner, listen to me. Five Points' encryption is secure. It has to be an organic leak, and she's the only variable."

"A rat explains a whole universe of things, but so would system infiltration." Conner smiled, but his eyes were cold and hard.

"Don't be an idiot. I know you're sharing her bed, but that doesn't make me wrong about this." Nikkei searched for a light, friendly tone. He failed.

Conner lifted the hand cannon from his pocket. The old, heavy gun glittered in the dim light. Susan had shot a few drones with it on their first date, and the damn thing nearly broke her wrist. As Nikkei stared at Conner, she flicked her Beretta to *On*; its centrifuge spun up with a mechanical whir just audible over the road noise.

"Put the itty-bitty pop gun back in your pocket, and let's talk this out." Conner didn't shout and was all the more menacing for that.

No one spoke. The truck rattled, electric motor whining like a bandsaw below them.

"Ten minutes to delivery," the tablet said in a creamy British accent.

A Transmission Digital ebook.
Ebook first published in 2020 by TRANSMISSION DIGITAL
Copyright © Jim Keen 2020

All rights reserved.

All the characters in the book are fictitious, and any resemblance to actual persons living or dead is purely coincidental.

Printed in Great Britain
by Amazon